Run With the Hunted 6:

Burned Asset

By Jennifer R. Donohue

I0457456

Run with the Hunted © 2023 by Jennifer R. Donohue

ebook ISBN: 978-1-945548-24-6

paperback ISBN: 978-1-945548-25-3

For Jim

1

Chapter One

The thing about countries that don't have extradition treaties with the U.S. is that they might still do it anyway. Especially if they got somebody they wanna trade, or at least something else to leverage. We only stayed in Mexico for a week or so, time enough to arrange transport to Morocco by way of Hong Kong and picking up Butler as additional insurance, just in case Will's usual terror of me wasn't enough to keep him well behaved during global travel.

He was fine, though. Docile, maybe stunned by what the fuck just happened to him. We didn't even drug him this time. Butler's happy enough to be along for a trip, though, and I more'n like the idea of having him for backup in case the agency comes for Will in force. Bristol can handle herself surprisingly well in certain situations, and even Bits is a great shot, but they've never been operators. If we're going to have some movie siege in Bristol's Moroccan hotel, I want somebody else who's done exactly that kind of thing more than once, from either side of the map.

I want more than just Butler, but once we land in Morocco and get to Bristol's hotel, all of the stress about what just happened and how we have to plan and anticipate moving forward just...melts out of her pretty little head. It's wild to watch, I look at Bits to see if she's catching it, but she's distracted and I don't want to break her concentration.

Bristol links arms with Will, chattering about the renovations or restorations or something that she did to the building.

"Bristles, we gotta set up a war room," I say, and she smiles at me over her shoulder.

"It's too early to even consider anything a problem yet, darling," she says.

"Way I see it, you're walking next to the problem and he's about six feet tall."

"Mmm, indeed. Tell us, Will, when were you scheduled to check in?"

"What's today's date?" he asks, sounding like a sleepwalker, and she shows him her watch. "Three days from now."

"See? No problem yet "

I look at Bits again, who is paying attention now, though who can say when she started. "Bristol, that's—" she starts.

"Let's just all get settled in," she says, and she click-clacks off with Will in tow.

"I guess she's never had a pet," Butler grumbles, and I laugh.

"Just. Fuck," I say, and light a cigarette.

"You know she—" Bits says.

"Yeah, yeah, I know." Bristol takes bad things that happen and puts little protective coatings around them, like an oyster making pearls. Who doesn't, right? But this isn't a bad thing that happened, this is a lull in an ongoing situation. "I'll call Nicolai, anyway, she can't object to him."

"I mean, she can." Bits pops the top on a can of coffee and looks around at the parking lot courtyard area. A couple other cars here, staff and whoever else Bristol just lets stay here. What was her friend's name? Suzette. "I think she likes him though."

"How can you tell?" Butler asks, sarcastic but not.

"She added him to her phone," Bits says.

"That's just a thing you do when you meet people," he says, and Bits blinks at him. "She didn't add me to her phone?"

"No."

"Well." He seems genuinely surprised and I laugh. "I think we're getting away from the point."

"I think we're all too tired to know what the point is," I say, dropping my cigarette butt and stretching. "Which is a problem."

"I'm good, if you two want to sleep," Bits says. "And I'll message Nicolai. And keep an eye on Will and Bristol."

"Thanks, Bitsy." I'm sure Bristol isn't about to put us all at more risk than she already just did, but takin' Will with us was kind of an elegant solution. Even though he's an agency asset, assets tend to be negotiable. Maybe they'll make a deal and cut their losses, cutting him loose. He was why they kept after us, mostly, and Bits said he was the one most into it.

Or maybe they'll come for him, with whatever black ops they got, and we'll have to assume that if whatever happens here gets written about on account of the explosions and whatnot, it'll be written off as a gas leak or something else equally un-noteable on an international scale.

Or we'll fake his death and set him up with a new identity or somethin', maybe she's got a plastic surgeon we can fly in, and that'll make this all real easy, no lead poisoning required. I like that one, honestly, maybe I'll float it at brunch or whatever. Over mimosas.

We've been here at the hotel before, not long after Bristol bought it, or more like after Bristol paid it off and before all the renovations after we took the money and ran way back when. The first time we came here, she was almost embarrassed, and called it 'shabby chic' even though it still seemed awful nice to me. Of course now, seeing the restored tiles and fresh paint and window dressings and other folderol, I can see what her problem was. But it was still nice the first time.

It isn't *really* a hotel, like strangers can't make reservations and stay here, but if you know Bristol, and Bristol knows a lot of folks, there's kind of an invite system I guess. Bits made sure of the tech security and all that, the discreet cameras and places where things need to be locked right and all of that. Much as Bristol wants to show off that fucking Fabergé egg, it can't become public knowledge that she has it, and she's smart enough to know that.

"You okay?" Butler asks, as we wander through the place to where I assume Bristol'd like to keep us.

"Hard to shake the idea that this is a mistake."

"You ran your options," he says. "I'm sure it'll be a ride, but we'll come out okay."

"Probably," I say. "You still got your lucky rabbit's foot?"

He laughs, and I realize we've been checking doorways as we passed them, even though neither of us is carrying a weapon at ready. "Surprised you remember that."

I shrug. "I remember a lot of things."

"Sometimes you don't act like it." Oh this again. Well what did I expect, I guess.

"Mmm," I say instead, knocking on and then opening the door to the room I had last time. I don't want to assume that I have a 'my room' at Bristol's fancy personal hotel for her fancy friends, but it doesn't look like a whole lot, if anything, changed in here. There's a tented card on the dresser, like a place setting, that says *Dolly*. That's Bristol, always prepared. "Well this is me."

Butler kisses the back of my neck. "Want company?"

"I want *sleep*," I say. "Maybe company in about sixteen hours."

"You'll never sleep that long." He's still very close. This is very tempting.

"Maybe not." I turn around, standing in the doorway. "She probably put you across the hall there, if you wanna check. If she didn't, you can stay."

"It amazes me that she'd even take the time to what, message ahead? To assign us rooms?" He goes and checks. "Yeah, I got a card in here too.

"It amazes me that it amazes you," I say. "See you later."

"Sweet dreams."

Tempting as it is, though, to just drop my boots on the floor and lay down in that nice clean bed, I go into the bathroom first, and of course the shower is stocked with shampoo and conditioner and perfumed soaps and all that and suddenly a hot shower and a cold beer is what I want first more than anything in the world and while I'm not sure that Bristol is exactly sold on the notion of shower beers, there is a mini fridge in the room, and it does have beer and canned coffee and water in it, so I'm all set.

I stand in the hot spray for a while, just letting the travel dirt rinse away, drinking my beer and trying to relax. It's funny the way that kind of long haul travel makes you tired and wired, even without the added bonus of stealing an agent from an un-named shadow agency. It was pretty clear he was done the second he saw Bristol in that hotel room when we stole the diamonds, but it's sure been a slow burn. Hard to blame him.

I finish the beer, then soap up and rinse off. There's a robe hung up in here that seems like it's probably worth more than cars I've driven. Not bought, mind you. But driven.

I get from the bathroom to the bed and that's what I remember for probably a good eight hours, which isn't enough but it's a start. I haven't spent enough time in Morocco to be able to tell what time it is from the light coming in the window and I slap around at the nightstand until I find my phone. Lots of messages but none of them dire; in addition to usual sorts of spam and people checking in from afar, Bits gave a couple of updates. No local law enforcement contact, no relevant chatter on the Agency network yet, that she's seen, Nicolai inbound probably tomorrow. Marquis also inbound in the next few days, which really just confirms my worries. Or is that a brilliant smokescreen, for Bristol to get the party started here, the way she normally would? No idea. Maybe it's both.

//I'm up, if you wanna turn in// I message Bits.

//I napped// she says.

//Liar// I roll out of bed and pull one of the coffee cans out of the fridge. If this was a real hotel, my tab would already be horrible. I chug it, then paw around in my clothes until I find both a tank top and pants, and get dressed. I jam my feet into my boots, then pause at the door, go back and put a bra on too. I don't need to have that conversation with Bristol first thing.

I wonder if Bristol's gonna want to pull some kind of designer bodyguard nonsense, like at the wedding gig. We'll get to it I'm sure. She's probably got a tailor on the way already. Or on staff. I open another canned coffee.

Chapter Two

———

When I listen at his door, Butler's still snoring, so I just leave him be and go wandering through the halls, savoring that canned coffee instead of shotgunning it, listening to my lace-ends clatter on the floor. Thinking about how this place has good, thick walls; we might not actually be fucked, if we have a siege.

There'll be fresh-brewed coffee, probably even the Turkish stuff Bristol loves so much; I think she keeps somebody on staff just to make that, and then read the grinds when you're done. She's quirkily superstitious, but also pays actual traditional practitioners of things, so I guess that's the way to do it.

As if summoned by my bootlaces, Bristol finds me. She already redid her manicure and pedicure, and whatever she does to her hair that makes it all sleek. Never in my life has my hair looked like that. No travel weariness evident here. "Really, Dolly darling, those laces are *awful*," she says, but smiling, like it isn't criticism.

"Sorry Bristles," I say, craning my head back to finish the coffee.

"You aren't."

"No," I agree. She plucks the can from my fingers before I can even look around for a bin. "That was one of yours, it's not like

I brought contraband canned coffee from a convenience store that's under your minimum acceptable price point."

"I know it's one of mine." She rakes me over with an appraising gaze. "I assume we'll want to meet? Have a plan? Can that be soon?"

"Got someplace to be?" I make a show of looking around. "Oh, you wanna do it while Will is still snoring."

"I assume he's still sleeping, yes," she says stiffly.

"Oh don't be like that, I didn't mean you spent the night with him. I know from that experience that Butler snores, but I can hear him from the hallway. Unless, of course, he recorded it to fool any onlookers and then went for a walk."

"So far as I know, he did not. Security would've alerted me."

"You've got a team?" News to me.

"In a manner of speaking." She smiles, happy to have a little secret.

"You can brief us in the meeting," I say, watching her face. Ah, Bits knows. I won't worry too much then. "Feed us, too."

"I expected you'd say that. Do you remember where the breakfast room is?" She's still smiling; she knows I remember how to get anywhere I've been.

I laugh. "I'm sure I can find it."

"Splendid, we'll meet in ten minutes." She looks at my untied boots again, and then swans off with my empty can. I don't know if what she's wearing is her version of a bathrobe or a beach coverup or if it's an outfit itself, layers of gauzy stuff that manages to never actually be transparent, more's the pity.

That look meant she wanted me to get changed, in addition to tying my boots, but I'm not doing that. What else am I gonna wear? //Bitsy, where you at?//

She doesn't answer right away, and I'm debating between being worried and assuming she actually finally fell asleep and then she says //Shower, sorry. //

//Meeting in the breakfast room in ten with Bristol.//

//It was that easy?//

//Yeah, but I'm also gonna assume no.// The vibe is off, I don't know. I go find a courtyard doorway to stand in on the way to the breakfast room and smoke my ecigarette for a few minutes. I'll pick up more real cigarettes later or tomorrow, probably. Sugar cookies ain't gonna cut it.

A couple things are true at once; if Bristol wasn't attached to him, it would've been easy to put a bullet in Will's ear a long time ago and maybe we wouldn't have this problem now, but also I don't regret taking him. It might've been Bristol's long game all along, not like she shared it with the rest of the class. I sure was surprised in Vegas when she said shoot him or let him go. Well, meaning bring him with us. There were more players involved at the time, of course, but Will was the one who mattered.

I go the rest of the way to the breakfast room, where coffee is out, and also what looks like a full English breakfast. Bristol click-clacks in not long after me; even her sandals have heels. "I assumed you would be absolutely ravenous," she says.

"Always am," I say. Bits comes slouching in and blinks at all the food.

"I wasn't expecting all of this," she says.

"Eat what you'd like, it doesn't matter," Bristol says, waving her hand as she settles herself at the table. "It won't go to waste, I mean," she adds, looking at Bits again. I didn't see Bits's face change at all, but that's Bristol's specialty.

"Okay," she says dubiously, adding sugar to her coffee.

"So Bristol, you got a plan, or are we—"

"Dolly, we've hardly had coffee," Bristol says serenely.

"Speak for yourself." But I watch her add her cream, and sugar before I try again. "Plus, if we're banking on finishing this conversation when it's just the three of us, we need to get to it before our, uh, guests are awake."

"We won't be interrupted," she says. I glance at Bits, who shrugs just slightly.

"Trained Suzette in the art of distraction, did you?" Bristol's got so many little party people, that's the only name I can remember, other than Marquis of course.

Bristol waves a hand. "Oh, Suzette's in Paris right now. She'll be back tomorrow, though."

"We're gonna be expecting a lot more than Suzette pretty soon," I say. "We got two more days before Will is supposed to check in and then—"

"And we just spent three days doing Bits's little game," Bristol interrupts. "And now we will spend three days my way."

"Bristol, I don't think that completely unplugging for three days is a great plan," Bits says. "Like, it's not a matter of whose turn it is to choose what to do? We're against a clock here, and right now we're the ones who know it's running, which is great. We need to take advantage of that."

"Once Will misses his contact window, they'll have a plan that goes into immediate effect," I say. "He's got clearances that they just can't let walk."

"Bits did a very good job covering our trail, I'm certain of it. Didn't you, darling?"

"I did my best, anyway," Bits says.

"And your own contingencies will tell us when they're getting close, won't they?"

"Well, I hope so. But—"

"See? We have time to relax and unwind, and come up with something. And then it will be Dolly's turn for us to do what she wants." Bristol pushes away from the table, smiles at us, and click-clacks away again.

Bits and I sit there looking at each other for a minute, and then she drinks some more of her coffee and I start in on the breakfast. "I guess I expected that," I say eventually.

"I didn't but I did, if that makes sense?"

"It does. I'd say I don't know what was wrong with her, but I think that she reaches a point where everything gets piled up and she just puts it down someplace and walks away. Like she doesn't want to think about commandos coming here to gun us all down or whatever, so she just doesn't."

"Bristol's smarter than that," Bits says cautiously.

"Sure she is, but..." I think I have more eggs than Bits and that can only be on purpose.

"But she does set really hard partitions between some things."

"Yeah, that's more it. She never expected to have to like, *work* here, so. She isn't." I kinda wave my hands around to express the nothing.

"Yup."

I drink some of my own coffee. "Oh, so what's going about security here? She was giving me smug, knowing looks and I figured you had it handled."

"It's almost totally surveillance and electronic things," she says. "And a couple of local kids who aren't trained, really, but are in love with her. A supervisor."

"Everybody's in love with her," I mutter. "Okay so that's a project. Or, I'll run 'em off so we aren't getting any nineteen year olds killed here. They're fine for off-season work." I think a minute, as Bits pours her next cup of coffee. "What do you mean, electronic things?"

"Cameras, of course. Some ingress/egress failsafes, if we're in a panic button sort of situation. Then some other things I've been messing with, like drones. Oh, and robot dogs. Not like your kind, the kind that don't have faces."

"Leave it to Bristol to have the robot dogs that *don't* have faces. How many are there?"

"Three." I nod, thinking about the property. That's an okay patrol amount. It's enough to overwhelm anybody who doesn't know how to handle them. "Anyway, I'll set the clearances so you've got full run of all of it. Will Butler want anything like that?"

"Probably a good idea, but god, how he hates robot dogs." I grin. "Both kinds." Bits laughs.

"Noted."

"You wanna come with me to get cigarettes before we bunker down?"

She pauses long enough that I think she's figuring out the best way to tell me that isn't the saying, or no and I shouldn't go either, but then says, "Yeah, let me find a place that actually sells cigarettes."

"I wasn't gonna make you do that." It's smart, though, I was just gonna drive around but I also know that we should minimize our off site activities.

"I know, but there isn't a 7-Eleven, so this will just make it easier."

I laugh. "Am I really that predictable?"

"Mmm." She finishes her coffee. "Okay, I found a 24 hour one."

"Bitsy it's like, nine in the morning."

She gives a little huff. "I know, I'm just saying."

"I'm pulling your leg, that's good to know. " I get up, slapping my pockets for keys like I need 'em.

"Should we touch base with anybody?"

"Butler's sleeping, and I don't care about Will, so, no."

———————

Traffic's okay but also I don't remember what day it is so don't know what to expect. Is it even tourist season? Is there a lot of 9-5 business here? Who knows. Bits seems to be actually looking at the sights out the window, and it is a nice day,

blue skies, hot already. They got both city buses and slick looking cable cars here, so that probably cuts down on passenger vehicles. Plenty of pedestrians and people on motorcycles with no
fear of man or meeting God, but where don't you see that, really?

Lotta places are still shuttered, which makes Bits's comment
about the 24 hour convenience store make more sense but it
could just be the approach I took, these are places that open and
close later. I notice surveillance, but it's heavier in some places,
nonexistent in others, and that's interesting.

We pass a smoke shop and a vape shop, but really, I prefer convenience stores and so does Bitsy. I also eye a McDonald's but we
did just eat. We try to be unobtrusive in the convenience store,
or, well, I try and Bits just *is* unobtrusive. I browse around the
snacks, the baseline for chocolate is always higher quality when
you're not stateside. The cigarettes have less advertising on them
and bigger warnings and I wasn't gonna get a carton but then I
think about the situation and I get a carton.

The guys behind the counter are doing the shift change and I
wait, watching traffic out the window. Bits comes up with an
armful of silver energy drink cans and when she drops one I
catch it before it gets too far. "Power Horse?"

"I've heard of it but never had it."

I realize the guys behind the counter are now looking at us, either because of our accents or because of how fast I just moved.
It's too early in the shift for one guy to see wild shit, and too late

for the other one, the thresholds are all wrong. They ring us up and as I realize I don't have any local currency, Bitsy produces a Moroccan bank card outta nowhere and taps it. The morning guy puts our stuff in paper bags, wordlessly, and the night guy doesn't say much of anything, just runs the register, and I manage not to laugh at them until we're back in the car again. It's not a big deal, it's not their fault. They should be thankful that they didn't have to mop up Power Horse this late in the morning and/or this late in the shift. I sure didn't want it on my boots.

Chapter Three

When Butler opens his door, he looks disappointed that I'm dressed and happy that I'm holding a coffee pot and a mug. Bits offered Power Horses for him, and myself, and I respectfully declined. "You let me sleep in."

"Girl talk," I say, shoving the mug into his hands and going into the room past him.

"Of course, what was I thinking." He closes the door and follows me. "We got a plan?"

"Of course not," I say and he does an honest to god double take.

"What?"

"Well, because we were just doing the game because it's what Bits wanted to do, Bristol is now taking her turn to do what she wants to do."

He rubs the back of his head. "What?"

I sit on the edge of the bed. "So, the security here is a coupla local kids that we either need to furlough or train up, and Bits has the surveillance and stuff all sewed up."

"I would expect nothing less." He drinks his coffee, watching me.

"Oh yeah, and robot dogs."

"I fuckin' hate robot dogs."

"Yeah, I know, it's fine. You won't have to deal with them." He stares at me, then drinks more coffee.

"Dolly..."

"You think I don't know? Anyway, they've never yet traced Bristol here, that we know of, and Bits erased and overwrote and threw off our trail best she knows how, and she's real damn good."

"She is, yes." He holds out his mug and I refill it. "You're not worried? You don't seem worried."

"When do I ever seem worried?"

"Point, I guess."

"Bitsy'll be able to give us an advance warning, even if all it looks like she's doing is stargazing. She'll know what to expect when, and we can shore up here but expect to cut 'em off someplace else."

"But we won't know what to expect? You've been dealing with these guys for a few years now."

"We've been having a mostly-cold shadow conflict for a few years, anytime we've dealt with them after the first time, it's really only been individuals. Will. That hacker once. The only time we ever saw anybody en masse was for the submarine and—"

"The *submarine*?"

"I told you about the submarine." I reach over and put the coffee pot on the dresser. "Anyway we're not really sure of numbers but the numbers've never been big. And they always try to be covert, because anything they're doing seems to have always been extra-judicial. They're not gonna want official local involvement."

"Well, as long as nobody accidentally tips off anybody to the pretty blonde rich lady who owns an entire fucking oceanfront hotel that she parties in..."

"Exactly, simple stuff." I grin at him, and we both laugh. "So we do a perimeter and make our shopping list if we need a shopping list and Bits keeps on keepin' on. Well we did go get cigarettes and weird French energy drinks so we're probably set for shopping. Nicolai gets in tomorrow."

Butler finishes his second cup of coffee, sets it down next to the pot. "Can we assume he'll bring some goodies?"

"When hasn't he?" I nod at the duffle bag Butler brought. "Though why don't you show me the goodies you brought?"

"What makes you think that's anything but a tuxedo so that Bristol doesn't skin me for being within smelling distance of one of her parties?"

"Heard the gunstocks clackin."

"No you didn't," he says, grinning, but he puts the duffle on the bed next to me. "That's the nice thing about private flights with rich women, you just get out on the tarmac and can bring a small arsenal."

"Sure is a perk." I run the zipper back and give a peek inside. I know he's just got his handgun strapped, so do I, but he's got a couple little ones too, I recognize the lockbox. A couple of the stocks I see are 3D printed and I raise an eyebrow at him; he knows what I think about 3D printed guns.

"Wasn't sure what we'd need, and figured it'd be fine enough in the environment short term. Takes 7.62, easy enough to source."

"Wouldn't it be funny if the rest of us are buckling down like this, and Bristol's the one who's right to just cut loose and not worry about it?"

"It'd be nice," Butler rumbles. "But—"

"Not holding my breath, don't worry about that." He's got optics in his retinal replacements, no need to worry about packaging scopes so they don't get knocked around too bad in transit, that was always such a bitch.

"What're the boys doing while you're gone?"

"Finishing up a chopper for customer pickup. They wanted a custom paint job, which Meatball's great at. He does people's street racers too, they fly him out everywhere for that."

"Well that's nice." I know that look he's got on his face; he doesn't want to talk about Scooter and Meatball. He almost doesn't want to talk about guns, which sure is a thing for us. No,

I'm pretty sure he's gonna propose again and is picking the time. Which is fine, it's not like I don't love him, but the timing ain't exactly great. I think I'm the one who asked the first time, and he'd been smart enough to know we were way too young. I don't think he'll do it this morning, anyway. I'd bet on it being within a week, except I'll probably keep the suspicion to myself so I don't have anybody to bet with. "Want to take our walk now, or do you want breakfast?"

"Haven't been up long enough for breakfast, let's have a look at the place."

The nice thing about party lights being strung up in the courtyards and gardens and whatnots is that it doesn't actually leave many shadowy areas for covert insert. At least not en masse; I'm thinking it'd be fun to try to do it, just to see if I can, without the active camo. I don't think they're liable to have it, what with budget constraints and all. Of course, they might get some inter-agency action if they admit that they lost an agent and want him back. Or maybe they'll just send somebody to kill him. I like thinking on the possibilities, and know if Bits sees anything she thinks is concrete, she'll share. Calm and thorough, Bitsy is.

We meet Bristol's local security team when we're looking at all the entry points, like actual gates, in the wall around this place. It *is* a pair of nineteen year olds, maybe they're twenty, maybe they're cousins. I've seen an older woman around too, so I'm not sure what *her* deal is yet. If she's a guest or another member of

Bristol's staff or what. The staff largely make themselves invisible, which is a little weird. I guess this might be a cushy place to work, make a couple meals a day, eat what you want, keep your mouth shut. I know Bristol tips good, I'm sure she pays good too.

"I'm Joker," the first one says, holding out his hand to shake. I do, but he must've seen something in my face, or been used to getting questions. He's got a good grip, and he's surprised at mine; they always are. "Like from a deck of cards. Bristol said we should have work names."

"I'm Floyd," the other one says. They both really want to be taken seriously, but have different ideas of what seriously is, I think. They're about the same middling height, dark hair cut shortish, in pants and polo shirts, that Bristol must've designated as uniforms. "We already talked to Bits."

"Did you now," I say. They're both carrying, and I'm itching to know what they've got and how many, if any, range hours they have. "Range hours" in the loosest sense of the word, I want to know about *experience* and also I want to just send them home and I can't do that without pissing Bristol off and really damaging their confidence. We might not need them, it might be fine, but also the idea of having a pair of the greenest of the green to have to maybe watch my back isn't great. "Did she tell you that you might see some action?"

"She did," Floyd says, and before he can continue, we're joined by that older woman I'd seen.

"She wasn't able to tell us what kind of action or how much," the woman says, holding out her hand. "Marge. I know you're Dolly."

"Sure am. This is Butler." She shakes, and I grin when we match grips. "You're also on security?"

"Head of security, such as it is." She glances at Joker and Floyd. Her hair is short, iron gray, and her accent is Dutch maybe. "What *are* we looking at? On a scale of, say, Waco to—"

"Nah, Bits wasn't bullshitting you, we don't know yet. She's got fingers in pies they don't even know they have." Well that metaphor got away from me. "Once they're moving anything, anybody, we'll know. I know it sucks, we're not happy about it either." Pretty sure that I know better than to hope for a non-response. It'd probably hurt Will's feelings, anyway, unless they *are* just a 'disavow' agency and we didn't have that piece of the puzzle. I'll bring it up.

"When I talked to Bristol, she just laughed and waved her hands and said 'we're having *parties*, Marge, you've always been able to handle those' and walked away."

It's a good Bristol impression, and I laugh. "Yeah, sounds right." She seems old enough to know better than to get caught up in Bristol's bullshit. Or maybe that's exactly it, she sees through it, sees something there that she wants to protect. "Sorry about all this."

"At least it pays good," Marge says, a little grimly. She's strapped too, of course, and the kind of comfortable with it that me and Butler are. Well okay, if she's been in charge of these boys, she's made sure they're trained. Maybe.

"I don't suppose the princess told you when the first party is," Butler says.

"Didn't she tell *you*? Tonight, of course." Marge doesn't roll her eyes but I think we understand each other. "Anyway, let me know if you need anything, you've got run of the place of course. Bristol said that too."

"Glad you understand," I say, and Marge matches my smile.

"Even if I didn't on her say-so, I would after meeting you." She gives Butler a nod and saunters off.

"That make you feel better?" he asks me.

"No, but sorta. Havin' a crystal ball would make me feel better."

"Those burn people's houses down if they're not careful."

I give him a shove, but I laugh. "You know what I mean."

"Much as anybody can, yeah."

"I'm an open book."

"Sure." We're at another gate, looking at the beach, and I picture our own ridiculous mini Normandy. Well, us as the defenders. I think it's more likely it'll be like, a six person team who inserts, from what we know of their style. They'll probably even use one of those goddamn parties as their cover, it's hard to imagine otherwise actually, and I gotta assume Bits is vetting guest lists as soon as she can get her digital fingers on them. The way Bristol's parties go, though, Bits'll have her work cut out for her, haring off after every friend of a friend who gets the word passed that there's an event. Bristol always wants too much attention. Every job we've ever done, Bristol wants too much attention.

It wouldn't be a bad approach, if we coordinated it that way. Having a series of glitzy, internationally attended parties could be just the thing, seein' as how the agency presumably can't just go barging wherever it wants, interfering with everybody. This'll make them have to work harder, which is smart on Bristol's part. Again, if it's intentional. Thing is, Bristol is always up for a party.

"Well, we've always been good at reacting," I say. "The more involved the plan is, the more there is to forget."

"True enough," Butler says, watching me. "Priority is you three first, and then Will."

"Well aren't you sweet," I say.

"Am I wrong?"

"No." We keep walking, come around to the parking lot again. Bits has all kinds of cameras set up, and I'm pretty good at spotting them, but I know there are a few I've missed. Good, that means other people will miss them too. "Right, so the plan is there is no plan, which I'm not in love with."

"It is what it is. We've come through tough spots."

"Sure have," I say. Thinking of my fancy replacement arm. Thinking of 'training' situations me and Butler and the rest of the guys were in, in the program, that were clearly real to everybody else involved. Some of those details are hazy, that's what being decommissioned and then illegally deprogrammed'll do for you, but live fire tends to stick with you. "I'm not used to second guessing myself. You think that's enough?"

"It'll have to be." He hesitates, and before he makes up his mind to do whatever he's thinking about, Bristol appears in the entryway. I think she's already wearing different clothes from this morning.

"Would one of you darlings mind going to get Marquis at the airport? Their usual car service is having troubles and the wait is just *so* long for the other ones, without advance booking."

"Yeah, I don't mind," Butler says.

"Let me take your picture, so they'll know they can trust you."

"I'm not sure I'd go that far," I say, laughing, and Butler laughs too.

"Trust is just one of those things," he says. "Where's Prince Charming, anyway?"

"Will is having breakfast," Bristol says, smiling in her particular, magnanimous way that shows she isn't stooping to our level.

"Should I have somebody bring out coffee for you, to take with?"

"Nah, I already had coffee service," he says, looking at me, then goes and gets in the car.

"If you see Nicky, grab him too," I call after him, and he waves a hand over his head without turning around.

"Dolly, don't yell," Bristol says, and disappears back into the hotel.

Chapter Four

With Butler gone for the moment, I go over the property again. Not with any specific, directed purpose, I just pick a direction to wander in. It's not a big enough place to get lost in, with or without built in direction sense, but I want to see if there's anything I might've missed, that I might notice if I'm not paying hard attention. It's hard to trick yourself into seeing a place new again, and it might not work, but still I try.

My bootlaces are still untied and I don't take particular care with other noise I might make besides, and the staff uses that to make themselves scarce ahead of me. I only hear one person scrambling, and don't laugh out loud at them, but it is funny. It's like belling the cat, I guess, but I belled myself.

Then I take a second to wonder, how *are* they making themselves invisible so easily? I stop and duck into a random room, one of like ten that're filled with plush furniture and gauzy curtains, and tie my boots. Then I get out my active camo box and turn the gadget on. It's always wild, watching my own self disappear; Bits always describes it in video game terms, like seeing pixels, and that's probably the best way to describe it, honestly. It's not environmental camo, like a ghillie suit or a tiger, it's something else.

I go creeping through the halls now, in the direction I'd heard that sudden scrambling, keeping my ears open. All is still as I reach a hallway junction and look down. Empty. But then, behind me, there's a click and a framed, full length mirror slides to one side, and one of Bristol's staff peers around and steps out. She looks youngish, maybe in her twenties, and is holding a tiny vacuum cleaner with an attachment at the end that almost looks like a feather duster. Makes sense, all these details and knicknacks, you need something like that I guess. Satisfied nobody's there, she moves further down the hallway, heading towards the room I just tied my boots in. There's another click, and I slip into the passage as the mirror slides back into place.

//Did you know this place has hidden goddamn passages?// I text Bits.

//No, I could never find blueprints. The records office had a fire ten years back.//

//Convenient.// Like, it's probably a coincidence, but...

//Wait why, where are you?//

//In a hidden passage, I thought that'd be obvious.// The floors have thick, plush carpets on them that look like the ones out in the hallways, and isn't that a Bristol-ass thing to do, have luxury fittings where the fewest people are likely to see them.

//Dolly.//

//It was behind a mirror. I was thinking about how funny it was that Bristol's staff were all making themselves scarce and then I was close enough to actually hear one making herself scarce and I took a second to wonder what was actually going on.//

//And then...//

//Well I tied my boots and popped the active camo and here we are. I'll wander around and get my bearings so I can draw you a map.//

She's quiet for a long time, and I start walking. There isn't any light in here, really, except what comes lancing through from cracks in the walls or whatever. I keep looking for peepholes that I think will be in a portrait, but then I realize that I don't think Bristol's got any portraits hung. Isn't that interesting. //Well we can use it to our advantage, anyway.//

//That's the idea.// I find a slightly glowing panel in the wall and stop to have a look. It's just a toggle switch, not a keypad or biometric or anything. Weird that Bristol would've kept this even from Bits. She has to know, though, it'd be even weirder if she didn't. Right? //She has to know, right?//

//What??// Oh maybe I left too much time in between there.

//Bristol has to know there's secret passages.//

//I assume yes.//

Fair enough. I listen for long enough to be sure nobody's outside wherever this hidden passage door will lead and toggle the switch. The click is very quiet, and the panel slides, and I'm looking at one of the guest bedrooms. This one doesn't have a little name card on the dresser, and the windows're still closed, so currently unassigned. I wonder if the passages lead to *all* the rooms, and I step out to have a look at the wall. There's gotta be a switch here too, or else what's the point?

I have to stop the panel from closing twice before I find it; it isn't on the other side of the wall from the switch in the passage. No, it's in the molding at the top of the bathroom door, which is about four steps away. Five if you're shorter than me, three if you're way taller. There aren't seams, it isn't really a *button*, it's just a place where when you touch it, it engages the mechanism. Somehow. Maybe they're all bluetooth or something. Magnets. I peek out the door to get my bearings; not the guest wing that me and Butler are currently housed in, but I think I'm oriented. I return to the passages, wait for that panel to close behind me.

A couple of times I hear staff and one time I press myself against the wall as an older guy with a toolbox comes past. He doesn't even miss a step; I won't call the passages roomy, but they're not tight either.

I wander around long enough that Butler gets back with Nicolai and Marquis. I've got a pretty good map of the place in my head by then. Map within a map. Not all bedrooms have the secret passage panels, which is good, because wow is that both creepy and dangerous. I don't want to accidentally merc one of Bristol's maids in my sleep. Kitchen, yes. Her Fabergé egg chamber, yes. I even find a panic room off one of the powder rooms by a main party area, and that makes me weirdly relieved, honestly. I take pictures of those controls and things and send them to Bits, who I assume has been tracking my movements through the depths of this place anyway.

I pop out into a hallway by the pool and saunter 'round to the front to say hey to Nicky. Marquis has already, I assume, gone to find Bristol and do air kisses and whatnot. Why there's a pool when the Mediterranean is right there, I'll never know. You'd think Bristol'd be horrified about the tolls that chlorine takes on the skin, but also the only time I've ever seen her swim was the time we took a header off a bridge in Macau. It's all, always, about appearances.

Nicolai and Butler are smoking cigarettes in the parking lot, Nicolai gesturing with his cigarette and speaking rapid Russian, Butler nodding. It takes me a second to catch up with what he's saying, I haven't thought Russian in a little while, but it's about caviar prices of all things, and sturgeon sustainability.

"Nicky I learned something about caviar lately, you'll be proud of me," I say in Russian, sidling up and taking Butler's cigarette to have a drag.

"I'm eager to hear it," he says.

"See, I didn't know caviar was like champagne, and it only meant wild sturgeon from *certain* places, I thought all sturgeon eggs were caviar. And then I heard that certain caviar was not only wild sturgeons from the Caspian and/or black sea *but also albino* and also a certain age. Fuck I forget what age." I give Butler his cigarette back. He takes it, but then he gives me a new pack of my very own. He must've done some duty-free shopping at the airport.

"I am...very proud," Nicolai says, and we all laugh.

"Did you get into the business? Bristol will be wild to hear it."

"I've got a share in a fishing vessel now, yes. I wanted to see how it might turn out. We do not fish the albinos, though."

"Still, diversifying the portfolio, good call."

"Thank you." He tilts his head and looks at me. "I think there might be cobwebs in your hair?"

"Better not be, Bristol would be horrified," I say, bending into one of the car mirrors to check. "Nope, just a thread." Must've been from one of the wall hangings or something.

"I thought it was your first gray hair, and I wasn't going to be the one who said anything," Butler says.

"Everybody always throws Nicolai under the bus," Nicky says with elaborate woe. "After sticking by each other through trouble and hardship."

"You're fine, buddy." I clap him on the shoulder. "Anyway, first party's tonight, are you excited?"

"I am, and also I must say, I'm proud of you for waiting this long before you asked what I brought you."

I grin at him. "Well that's for when we get inside. You had cigarette left."

"Dolly, you are always so kind," he says in English.

"She's right behind me, isn't she?" I ask, still in Russian, right before Bristol click-clacks out the front door and down the long low steps to the parking lot. Anyway, I can't hardly keep track of what *I* speak, much less what Bristol speaks.

"Nicolai, darling, how good of you to come!" she says, doing the partial embrace air kisses with him. He looks at me over her shoulder in silent desperation.

"How could I not?" he says smoothly. "If I missed this opportunity, you may never invite me again."

"Nonsense, darling, you've been *such* a good friend." Maybe she means that; Nicolai was the only help I could get when me and Bits had to spring Bristol from federal custody. If Butler was stateside, he would've come. If Bits had been in her right mind, she maybe could've had people to ask. Maybe not; those hacker types aren't always physically helpful.

Another presence behind me, Bristol's friend Suzette, who is much less stealthy. "Bristol, the wine delivery is here," she says. I look out at the parking lot; there is no truck.

"Thank you, darling, I'll be right there," Bristol says. She lays her hand on Nicolai's arm for a moment. "Just wait until you meet Will, I do think that you two are going to get along well!" and then she turns and breezes back past me, and I listen to her and Suzette's heels recede into the hotel.

Nicolai looks at me, and I shrug. "Will's pretty inoffensive," I say. "And probably needs deprogramming."

"That is outside my expertise," Nicolai says, and Butler laughs.

"I'm sure you'll take to it like a duck to water," he says.

"That saying does not make sense."

"Sure it does, Nicky," I say. "Much as anything else."

Chapter Five

Deprogramming Will is where Bits has been. He said from the get-go that he didn't have any programming, but that's the bitch of the posthypnotic suggestion shit of which our government has become so fond; sometimes there's stuff in there, walled off, that they made you forget that they walled off to begin with. We all got programming. We just don't all have government clearance programming, some of it's just the normal sorts of things like who goes at a four way stop and holding the door for the person coming inside behind you. Dolly, you might say, that's just living in a society. Maybe it is.

It's easy to assume, when you're in the club, that they aren't gonna do anything to you. It's also easy to sign employment-type contracts that you don't read or understand every word of, no matter how hard you try, your eyes glazing over, and then you figure, well, other people signed it, what's the worst? That's how you get yourself programmed. It's also, sometimes, how you get yourself out of whatever poverty rut your life was otherwise gonna take. Would I have signed up for that little secret government super soldier project if I knew what-all it was gonna be? Maybe not. Did the fact that I had brothers and friends who'd already signed up ahead of me nudge the needle? Sure did.

I don't *really* regret it; I don't think it changed who I am as a person, who I was going to become. And it's sure helped me out; if I didn't have my pain senses rescrambled, my adrenal systems and

39

what have you adjusted, I never would've made it out of there, gotten to the doc to get a cybernetic arm put on. I would've just gone into shock and bled out on the spot when my original arm got blown apart. So no, I don't regret still being here.

It's a nice room, they're all nice rooms, this one big and open and with doors or windows or windows that're doors looking out at the beach, long gauzy curtains blowing in the wind, cushions and art with a capital A all over the place. Will was looking pretty relaxed until he realized it was me who'd come in. He seems almost comfortable around Bits, which I guess makes sense. He's a puppydog for Bristol and has been since first sight, and he's scared of me, he can't hide that. But Bits, he isn't physically scared of or physically attracted to, he just knows that she's one of the best hackers in the world. And if she isn't one of the best hackers in the world, then we're *all* in trouble.

There's a pitcher of iced coffee on the low, carved table between them, with brass fittings on it, and cups on a tray on the table. Cups that're too small for Bitsy's particular coffee habit, but we must have appearances for appearances sake, in Bristol's realm. "How we doing?" I ask. What *is* the prim 'n' proper thing to say, when somebody's getting their brains preliminarily unscrambled? Well, I'm not being fair; any work Will had done to him was a light touch. He came primed eager to save the free world, after all.

"I think it won't take much more for us to be okay," Bits says, and Will blinks at her. "It's lucky I've got your files, it really made this easier, knowing the kinds of—"

"You didn't even do anything," Will says, as I plop down on the couch, which creaks warningly, and reach for an empty cup on the tray, and the coffee pot. Bristol's furniture is for show, not rough treatment, good to know.

"Sure I did," she says. "It's just hard to know what I changed, because you didn't know what was there in the first place."

"So you could also just be making this up to push me away from the agency and gain my trust," he says.

"I could," she agrees. "But what would be the point? If I was going to manipulate you, I'd just change your posthypnotic suggestions to not be able to hurt us or whatever. Betray us?" She looks at me, frowning a little.

"Yeah, that sounds a little too supervillain," I say. This coffee is black as tar, I don't know who made it or how they got it that way. There's no spoons on the table, maybe because they all dissolved. Will watches us, his face schooled blank. Bristol has him dressed in resort clothes somehow, linen pants and a short sleeved button down shirt that's just the right blue for his eyes. Unless he already had that packed in his luggage, but I've seen how Will dresses himself, and this ain't it.

"You can't claim you're not manipulating me," he says, in a meter that says he's trying to be honest while choosin' his words carefully. "I'm not really here voluntarily."

"You mean you didn't want an all-inclusive luxury getaway with the woman of your dreams and her accomplices?" I ask with a grin.

"That isn't—"

"Relax Will, Jesus. We're all Bristol's puppets, it's fine. Like yeah sure we've held you at gunpoint a coupla times, but she does really want you to want to be here, and that's the truth." The coffee's strong enough to knock you on your ass, and it takes a lot for *me* to say that. "Bitsy, should this be watered down or something?"

She shrugs and makes a noncommittal noise, frowning into the middle-distance at something. "What do you know about Bristol's friend Warrington?"

"Is that his first name or his last name?" She doesn't say anything. "Nothing, sounds like a British prep school old money guy."

"That's what I thought too. Just socialite things." She blinks again, looks at me. "You don't like the coffee?"

"It tastes fine, I just think it's maybe concentrated jet fuel that isn't meant to be drunk like this."

"Oh maybe." She looks at the pot, considering. "Anyway, Will, you're probably tired for the day?"

"I didn't assume I would be off the hook so easily," he says.

"Bristol wants to parade you around, if I exhaust you too much for that, she'll be upset."

"Parade me around?" I watch the realization dawn on Will's face. He's as aware of her proclivities as he can be, which means he knows about Bristol's party people. He knows about Bristol's parties. And he's just now considering the implications of his involvement in one of those parties. "Oh."

I laugh. "Yup," I say, tossing back the rest of my coffee. "Yeah, Bits, you really shouldn't be drinking this straight."

She shrugs, looking at something else again already, I'm sure. "It's fine. How's Nicolai?"

"Also fine. Brought us goodies, mostly of the not-online type."

"Just the way you like it."

"Exactly." Will's still sitting there like he doesn't know exactly what he should be doing; leaving to find Bristol, still talking to us, what. "Buddy, you got a question?"

He takes a beat and then kind of laughs. "I'm just lost," he says. He's cute, I'll give Bristol that, but also those corn fed good looks gotta hide a level of unexpected duplicity or else the agency never would've had him on in the first place.

"Yeah, that feeling'll probably be around awhile. Uh, let's see. I dunno how much to tell you about everybody, we're operating under the assumption that somebody'll come and try to steal you back." I'd also assume sooner rather than later, but so far we've got clear skies.

"It makes sense to keep things need to know," he says. Maybe he thinks that'll limit his culpability, if we don't just introduce him around to Nicolai the arms dealer and whoever else. He already met Marquis, back when.

"Glad you see it that way." Maybe he just thinks I won't put a round in the back of his head once things start to slide sideways, if he behaves. Might be I won't. "Anyway, let's bring you to find Bristol." We gotta talk about him being supervised, at our next meeting. Providin' there is a next meeting.

Bits pours another cup of jet fuel. "I'll be here if you need me," she says.

"I figured you were about due to become furniture," I say, and she laughs. "You flyin' anybody in to help us out?"

"I reached out to Lockhart but he's pretty nailed down still. Same with Charlie. I've got friends in other time zones who can help me keep track of things, though."

"You're just saying that so I assume you sleep at all."

"We don't lie to each other."

"Yeah maybe, but we also don't always tell the truth." She gives me a wry smile, and I laugh.

"You aren't kidding."

I could ask her where Bristol is, but it's more fun this way. I lead Will off down the halls, and he has the good sense to walk next to me. If there's a party tonight, Bristol probably won't have a real lunch planned, but there might be finger food someplace. Brunch. I dunno, sometimes she seems to exist on champagne and gossip, and I know that isn't true.

"One thing we've never been able to figure out is how the three of you came to work together," Will says abruptly, like he rehearsed it but couldn't figure out a better way to say it.

"Hoping to get some counterspying in?"

"At this point, no. So I'm just giving in to curiosity."

"I admire the honesty." Well he did just watch Bits and me talk about that; I wonder if that's new information for him, that we don't lie to each other. I wonder how he *feels* about it.

"Obviously you were in a program, but Bristol and Bits just come out of nowhere." He pauses and I wait; he's fighting that conditioning, and maybe surprised that he even said that much. "And don't take this the wrong way, but you and Bristol..."

"Don't seem like the type to associate?" The tips of his ears turn a little bit pink and I laugh. "First time I met Bristol, we got in a bar fight."

"You *what*?" This place's echoes are interesting, if you get enough volume, which Will just did.

"She was putting a team together." And I thought she was gonna get herself killed. I guess that remains to be seen.

"I guess that tracks." He doesn't believe me. Do I care?

"Why, what was your guess?"

"I don't know. Maybe that Bits found each of you?"

"Okay, not a bad thought." Bits *did* find us, but after we'd already hooked up. Met, I mean. Agreed to work together. "But no. Shittiest bar Bristol's ever set foot in before or since, I'm sure. In heels, with her hair up in the knives." I tip a grin at him and he frowns. "Bet that was a bad surprise."

"That whole situation was a bad surprise." He's quiet again and a few steps later, Bristol's laugh floats down a hallway towards us.

"There she is," I say. He's perked up already and probably doesn't even realize it. "Look, I need to know that you aren't going to fuck us," I say, grabbing him by the arm and keeping my voice low.

"Even if I wanted to, I couldn't," he says, going *very* still, which means he doesn't know if I have a weapon, if it's out already behind him, whatever, and has maybe thought about this a lot. "I'm almost certainly disavowed and all my points of contact shut down. But I...I don't want to. I'm not happy with how this happened, but I'm starting to feel glad that it did."

He's gotta be a better liar than he looks. But still, I believe him, and I let him go. "Maybe you'll regret that, but I hope not." I hope none of us regrets this more than we already do. It's kind of Bristol's ultimate triumph, now she's got that Fabergé egg *and* the handsome man she made take her to dinner in the middle of the diamonds disaster.

Chapter Six

———

I find some paper and draw a rough map of the hotel, and then a rough map of the secret passageways. Bits can screenshot it and then I can give it to Butler to memorize. Hell of a thing, for Bristol to have secret passages she didn't bother to tell us about. It's fine, she'll know we know eventually. We just won't mention it until it matters. Or until it's the funniest.

I figure none of us are invited to the party tonight except maybe Nicolai, so I'm not gonna worry about what I'm wearing, I worry about where I'm gonna be instead. Can't overuse the secret passages or that'll be a secret that gets unsecret real fast. I can hang out with Marge and the kids, get a sense of how they do things, and how they run the robot dogs, or not. Could've asked earlier, but I'd rather see it than have 'em explain it cold.

I hear the smear of voices as more people arrive, singly or in twos and threes, Bristol I'm sure going to meet each of them. She doesn't put any of them in rooms down here by me and Butler, yet. Bits is probably in this wing too, I haven't asked. I should. I'm starting to feel like a sheepdog that doesn't know where-all the flock is, and clamp down on that. Bristol's got that panic button she wears now. Bits is a literal thought away from communicating with us at all times. It's fine.

When I decide the party is in swing enough that I can insert in the fringes and it'll be fine, I open my door. I heard Butler go back to his room a ways back, I assume for a nap; he likes doing that for night ops, when he can. He's not long after me when I head down the hall, though. "Hoping to scrounge some dinner?" he asks.

"Bristol always has the best horse divorce at these things," I say.

"What."

"It drives her nuts if you say stuff like hors d'oeuvres wrong. Horse divorce. Canapes as canopies is another good one. Car shootery."

"For...charcuterie?"

"Got it in one. Now don't overdo it, it'll ruin the effect."

"Your secret's safe with me," he says, sounding mystified, though I don't know how he can possibly be surprised that I think it's fun and funny to needle her.

I give him a sidelong look when we get to the door, terrace full of Bristol's party friends just outside in the twinkle-lit darkness. "Anyway, where's your tux?"

"Gut told me tonight's not a tux night." He gives that slow sly grin that keeps me on the hook.

"Well fine, how 'bout your gut gets us some plates while I go see Marge."

"You got it." He steps outside and blends through the crowd, a hell of a thing for a man his build and stature to do, and a treat to watch every time. I don't know for sure where Marge will be, but I can guess where Marge would be, because it's where I would be, and I slink my way over there. Bingo.

"Is this about what you expected?" she asks once I'm standing next to her and we've surveyed the scene a second. Bristol's party friends are all physically beautiful, and either wearing lots of sparkle that you just know is expensive, or the kind of simplicity that you know is even more expensive.

"Pretty much exactly, yeah." I can't see Bristol in the crowd, but I can see the crowd's movements around her. "Maybe less people than I expected, but it's only the first day."

"Debating whether to let the dogs out to patrol," she says. "Outside the walls, not in with the guests."

"I think it's probably a good call," I say. "Mind if I come with?"

"Please do."

I can't even remember the first time I saw one of those robot dogs, they've just been a fixture in law enforcement and military and whatnot since before I was born. Bits has shown me some of the early videos, the stuff they used to worm it into the public consciousness, to charm them out of stopping and thinking, *wait a minute. What is this for? Why would this be for that?* I wonder if the people who invented, engineered them, whatever, ever regret it. They thought they were making like, agile hostile environment investigative equipment, not crowd control toys to put in the hands of some of the worst people.

I've seen them stored a number of ways; folded up like a suitcase and racked, not folded but stacked, or stabled, like how Marge has them. Easy access, I guess, and space isn't an issue. "How do you tell them apart?" I ask and Marge frowns at the robot dogs and then at me.

"Would I ever need to?"

"Well do you refer to 'em by number when they're loose or what?"

"We refer to them by area of operation."

"Oh that makes sense." It does. She's still looking at me and waiting, though. "Why don't we name them, and give them different patrol behaviors. That way, nobody's learning their patterns, but also won't expect deviations from normal programming either."

"How are we going to do that? Do you know how to program them?"

"A little, but Bits'll have that covered. Might already, actually."

//I'm working on it, but you'll have to name them, I'm bad at that.//

"Bits says we'll have to name them," I say to Marge, who nods impassively. Just confirms what I already assumed, that she's seen a lot. "Anyway, just throwin' a tablecloth on one of these is enough to keep them from messin' with you, unless they're modified." There's a moment where none of us say anything, and Marge shrugs. "Bits, are they modified?"

//Just the one. Uh.// One of the robot dogs stands up taller on its four legs, like it's stretching.

"Got it." Marge nods, looking from the robot dogs, to me, back towards the party. "Fill me in later on what I need to know."

"Will do." It's hard to tell if she thinks I'm fucking around, or if she's happy to be relieved of the robot dog responsibility. Both can be true.

———————

We kind of knew it would, but the evening passes without a hitch. I don't know who the attendees think Butler is, but they're weirdly charmed by his tall, dark, and handsome, and he can tell war stories and talk about helicopters, so he fits right in with some of the personalities Bristol's collected. I don't talk to many people but Marge and the boys; Bristol's guests are the type to assign a person to scenery pretty easily, and I don't want to dissuade them of that unless it's absolutely necessary. For that first party, it isn't.

At the end of the night, some guests split off to assigned rooms, and I'm sitting at a patio table sharing a bottle with Marge and Butler when Bristol wanders through. We'd sent Floyd and Joker home probably an hour ago, and I'm surprised to see Bristol; I thought she'd be having an even smaller party in the parlor or something with a whittled down chosen few.

She sits with us, though, and when I offer her a glass she nods. She seems tired, but pleased.

"A success?" I ask. Actually, I wonder what about her makes me think she seems tired. Might be useful to catalog.

"Very much so, thank you. Will Bits be joining us?"

"I think so." On cue, Bits comes through one of the open doors with the designed to be billowy curtains. "Yeah."

"Hi," Bits says, and Butler laughs. Bristol glances at him, smiling quizzically.

"It's just funny seeing you three mesh."

"We are a well-oiled machine," I say, sliding a glass over to Bits too, even though she'll probably only just sip it a little for the fellowship. She looks tired too, maybe she'll actually sleep for once. "Oh, speaking of, Bristles, we named the robot dogs. You don't mind, do you?"

She gives a little laugh. "I entirely forgot that I even *had* them, why would I mind?"

I shrug. "I dunno. People get a certain way about naming things."

She takes a sip from her glass, maybe thinking about that, maybe a million miles away, and then says "What did you name them?"

"Loki, Snorri, and Mr. Squeak but it's a girl."

"But...it's a girl?" She sets her glass down. I wonder if she practices frowning in a mirror, so it doesn't wrinkle her up too much.

"Yeah, I found a bow someplace and glued it on. Gives her character."

"To review, as I've forgotten...these are the patrol and security style of robot dog? Not the type that yours is?"

"Yeah, that's what they are."

Another pause, and then Bristol nods. "I understand, darling, thank you."

Marge laughs. "I told her I thought you'd like the bow," she says, finishing her drink. "I ought to be going, though."

"Thank you, Marge," Bristol says. I'm not sure if Marge is just eager to turn in, or if she's feeling Bristol close that loop of help versus not-help.

"Sure you don't want to hang around longer, trade some war stories?" I ask, grinning.

She hesitates, glancing at Bristol, who arches a brow. "I could be persuaded."

"I'm not so sure war stories are a good idea," Butler says.

"Oh yeah?" I ask.

"Yeah. Either Marge'll just cement her confidence in us as operators, or decide the best thing for her hide is to get away from us."

"Aw, I don't know about that," I say.

"Perhaps you *should* share a story, Butler," Bristol says, in a deliberately circumspect tone. "Dolly tells us so little about herself, and you."

"You never ask." I top off my drink, hold the bottle up, and Butler moves his glass over. Bits blinks at us like she can't decide if she's asleep or awake.

Butler clears his throat and looks at me; I shrug. I have no idea what story he has in mind. "So we're drinking whiskey, not tequila, but why don't I tell you a story about tequila," he says. Oh, this one. I knock back my glass without comment, and for some reason, that makes Bits look more awake. "Okay, this was when we were still in the program. Double black ops, even the secret projects don't know about us secret project, super soldiers in a base in Mexico. What are we doing in Mexico? I still don't know. Weren't supposed to be there, definitely. But we're in Mexico, on fucking dry base. Bored out of our minds, whole team just climbing the walls. Whatever action they had planned for us just wasn't happening."

Bristol is *very* intent; I have definitely never shared any detailed stories from the super soldier days. I'm not sure she'll love the payoff of this, though. "And what does a secret super soldier who isn't where they ought to be do in such a situation?" she asks. Bits smirks a little, but she doesn't know either. The level on her glass is lower than I expected, though.

"We're all on active duty, could be in the shit at any minute. Concertina wire, helmets, full armor. A million degrees down there in the jungle and we're sweating it out every day all kitted out. Maybe it's just a training exercise, and central is running some kind of test on us?" He pauses, just a little too long. "I guess technically everything they did was a test."

"But that's neither here nor there," I say, in my imitation of Bristol's voice, and she gives me a rueful look.

"You're right, it ain't. But so we hear stuff about the little town that's nearby, because what else is there to talk about? Not that the guys that are actually stationed there talk to us *much*, but they did enough that Dolly hears there's a special kind of tequila that they make here. Some bullshit magic mushroom tequila that I think they put scorpions in, instead of a worm, to scare the gringos."

"Do they even have scorpions, in Mexico?" Bristol asks.

"Mexico has lots of scorpions," Bits says. "I think the most in the world? No. The most *biodiversity* in scorpions in the world."

"...oh."

I look at Marge to see how she's taking all this in, and she's got one of those little smiles on that says she knows that this is a for fun bullshit story, and nothing too serious. Good. "Get to it, Butler."

"I'm setting the scene," he grumbles. "So Dolly goes, *solo* mind you, over the fence. Through the concertina wire, down to that town, where the bar is like, in some old lady's kitchen. Dolly, in her best Spanish, which is pretty good actually, asks for a bottle of magic mushroom scorpion tequila. The lady looks at this random American in her jungle and asks…"

"Plata or un año," I supply.

"Right, silver or one year. And Dolly, acting like she knows what the fuck this lady is talking about, says one year. Because, she reasons, older booze is better booze."

"I'm not wrong." Actually, looking at the label of this bottle of whiskey I've been so liberal with, it is not cheap whiskey. Bristol, to her credit, has not commented on that. Not that she tends to, actually. She hates to waste things, and sometimes wasting things is hoarding them away where nobody enjoys them. What's the point of liquor nobody drinks?

Butler laughs. "No, you're not, but I'm telling the story."

"It's not a very good story, really," I say to the table, and Bits laughs. "You're going to be underwhelmed. In fact, we might as well—"

"I want to hear it," Bristols says primly.

"Well. If the lady wants a story…" I light a cigarette, offer around the pack. Marge takes one, accepts the lighter.

"So she gets what, five? Six?" I nod. "Seis bottles of mezcal escórpioin un año, and starts her walk back out into the jungle, because that's always been a thing about Dolly, even before the super soldier stuff, she never gets lost. She'd taken her jacket and body armor off once she was outside of the fence, stashed them in a tree that was like, older than the world, so she wouldn't look like partisans or something coming out of the jungle. She gets back to the tree, and I'd say no sweat but like we mentioned, it's a bajillion degrees out, and as she's getting back in her jacket, she hears a noise."

"A noise?" Bristol asks, when he pauses for dramatic effect.

"A noise." He nods. Quite the storyteller, our Butler. "See, one of the guys there all the time, he tried to get us all spooked about chupacabras, but Dolly just wasn't having it. But in the middle of the jungle in the middle of the night, after maybe sampling some old lady's hallucinogenic tequila, you wonder. Dolly's checking the perimeter, making sure she's clear to sneak back in the way she came, but the noise is getting closer, and then she hears a radio nearby, an honest to goodness walkie, tuned way down low. And the action we'd all been waiting for, it was creeping up on the base right then."

"Well shit," Marge says, suitably impressed already. I guess it makes sense; I'm still here, right?

"So Dolly figures she needs to cop to what she's done because this is a bigger problem, messages the CO, but now these guys are between her and the fence, and she's got only a sidearm but also the drop on them, and *is* a secret supersoldier. But then Dolly feels something on the back of her neck."

Everybody looks at me, as if on cue. "I froze, because God knows what I've just encountered, and then I felt something on my arm too. It was fucking scorpions, because apparently where the scorpions in the tequila came from, for generations, was that super old tree. Dunno why. I don't know anything about scorpions, except apparently they love armored jackets when you give them the chance. Or loved *my* armored jacket, on account of how sweet I am. I didn't know how poisonous the things would be, what would make them sting, nothing. If they were real because yeah, I did get a sample of the tequila." I drag on my cigarette, shudder. That night had been beyond surreal. And ridiculous.

"So figuring she has nothing to lose, she whips off her jacket again and throws it over the head of one of the guys in the back, shoots two others, and then hit the dirt and prayed, I assume, as the lights on the base fences come on like the fucking sun and the teams assembled open up. Fucking bloodbath."

Bristol looks from Butler, to me. "That's the story?" she asks.

"I mean, I took a couple of rounds. I said it wasn't actually a very good story." I start to blow a smoke ring, but the breeze off the beach is a little too much. "One of the scars was in the arm I don't have anymore and the other one was fixed by Uncle Sam during one of the other surgeries. But no scorpions stung me, anyway, so jury's out on whether they were *actually* real, biodiversity or not."

"It's a great story to let people know how you are," Butler says.

"Sure it is, except there were shorter ones you could've employed. Like that time in Germany—"

Marge finishes her drink. "It's a fine story," she says. "I am going to turn in now, though."

"It is *very* late," Bristol says apologetically. "Much as I'd like to hear about Germany. Did that one also involve substances?"

"Nah, no hints," I say, before Butler can answer. I reach over and take his glass, finish the little bit he's got left. "Shuteye for all of us then, we'll leave the estate to the hounds." Mr. Squeak comes by on patrol at that moment, to illustrate my point. We all watch her go, the strings of lights glistening off the sequins on the bow I found. Marge gives her a little tap as she goes past; I wonder where she lives, actually. "I think she's a keeper," I say, once she's out of earshot.

"I'm very fond of Marge," Bristol says. "She does very well here, for me."

"Well good," I say, standing up and stretching until something in my back cracks. "Butler, shall we?"

"Sure," he says, a look of watchful intent in his eyes. He doesn't want to misunderstand.

"Goodnight, everybody," Bits says, and I grab her mostly-full glass before I go. I should've asked where Will is. Bits absolutely knows where Will is. Sorry he missed storytime, though.

Chapter Seven

The next morning, me and Bits sit down at the breakfast table but there's no place setting for Bristol, not even for coffee. "So much for the debrief," I say.

"You can't be surprised."

"I'm not surprised, just disappointed," I say, poking at the bowl of sliced fruit. Figs and melon and blueberries, and I wonder if Bristol okays a menu every day for the kitchen or what. Probably. I can't really imagine her just letting anybody else decide, this is her playground. Like how I'm sure every plant on the property has been examined and signed off on by her, not that I think she's a gardener, but because of the aesthetic vision.

"At least everything went fine last night," Bits says.

"Bitsy, you don't gotta try to make me feel better, I'm a big girl. And also we're still in the window of 'Will's people might think everything's still copacetic' so..."

She shrugs. "I know."

I squint at her. "*Do* they still think everything's copacetic?"

"Yeah, they seem to think so," she says, without hesitation.

"Have you *slept* since we got here?" It isn't fair to expect her to do round the clock crisis digital surveillance, we should've talked about this before we got here, or when we got here, or yesterday, or—

"Yeah, don't worry about it. I've had Speckle and Nautical Deborah doing dedicated tradeoffs, and a couple of others doing broader surveillance."

"Okay, good." We eat in silence for a few minutes. "Nautical Deborah?"

"She's in an oil platform squatter community." Bits is doing that look off and to the right thing, her eyes scanning just slightly, and I leave her be a little longer, chewing on that intel along with my breakfast.

"Is there a....what, Landlocked Deborah? Do you also have Zeppelin Steve?"

"No, I don't think any perpetual aerial communities have lasted long enough for anything like that," she says, then blinks and looks at me. "It's not that weird a name."

"Not really, and that's part of what makes it so weird, I think." Perpetual aerial communities. Sure. What do I know. "Anyway, I think we've in general hit the more normal end of hacker names. I haven't run into a whole lot of Zorgoth the Destroyers or whatever, and honestly I'm disappointed."

"Naming conventions shift every few years, there's still time."

"I would never make fun of Nautical Deborah to her face," I say.

"Well no, we'd have to go out there, and—" she looks at me, blinking more. "I know."

I laugh. "I think you need more sleep than you got."

"Probably, but..."

"Yeah."

Somebody's approaching from down the hallway, and Bits and I both look to the door as Nicolai appears. He glances in as he walks past, then stops and backs up. "You're up early," he says, a bit sheepishly.

"Nicky, you disappeared last night," I say. I saw him circulating early on, maybe right after we named the robot dogs, and then not after. "Coffee?"

"I had to take some calls," he says, coming to sit. "And then when I returned, I met a very nice woman who shared my interest in caviar."

"Your passion maybe?" I ask, and he smiles again.

"Maybe," he agrees."Such things are a flash in the pan."

"I don't know if that's—" Bits starts, and I cut her off.

"Yeah, they can be." Nicolai is very judicious about his one night stands, but they're always one night stands. Good for him, really; comin' from a big family like his, it's hard to guess if he's gonna abruptly settle down and have a million kids, or just be a perpetual bachelor. Or maybe that's what his caviar business is supposed to be, a nice, close to home step down from the arms dealing.

"Won't she be at the party tonight, though?" Bits asks.

Nicolai shrugs. "Maybe. And maybe we will again pass the time."

"Don't poison Bitsy's mind with your Casanova ways." I'd offer him some of my breakfast but I ate it. It's fine, I'm sure there's a nice buffet Bristol has for the real guests, like an all-inclusive resort.

"My apologies," he says, and she shakes her head.

"Dolly can't decide if I'm impressionable or not. We're all grown ups."

"Sure we are," I say. She isn't mad, just mystified. "Anyway, hear anything interesting on your end of things?"

"No, just normal party things. Not even a business lead. Most of these people Bristol has surrounded herself with are entirely careless. Without responsibility."

"Kinda like how Bristol herself wants to be," I say. "For one more day, at least."

"I beg your pardon," Nicky says.

"It's only fair," Bits says, and we laugh.

"I do not understand the joke."

"It's okay. Just keep your eyes peeled and your hands wandering, I guess." I push back from the table and stand up. "I might take another field trip, want anything from off site, Bitsy?"

"Not if it has scorpions in it," she says, and the face Nicolai makes is a combination between pleading and horrified.

"I'll tell you some other time, bud," I say. "Or actually, ask Butler, he tells it better."

"Maybe stay here, though," Bits says as I'm leaving the room.

"You might be right. Don't wanna trip the global surveillance network and give Nautical Deborah too much of a hard time."

Before I'm out of earshot, I hear Nicolai say "I know you aren't speaking in code, but it does not make it any more understandable."

═══════════

I run our perimeter again, what else am I going to do? Maybe I should be resting up. Once ops kick off, there isn't going to be much opportunity for that, why not just enjoy myself? But I actually don't trust that; I don't think Will was lying about his three day check in window, I think he believes it. But I think things're gonna be in motion tonight or tomorrow and if I'm wrong that's fine and if I'm right, nobody made any bets with me anyway.

Butler comes out to join me when I'm staring at the beach through one of those doors in the wall again. "Missed my coffee this morning," he says.

"Sorry, got distracted."

"Understandable." He's good at not smothering me, I appreciate that. "Any news?"

"Nothing. It's driving me nuts."

"It'd be a hell of a thing, if they just never came for him."

"Wouldn't it though? We'd never be able to trust that, though. Disavowed, or double cross?"

"Are you ever gonna trust him anyway?" He lights a cigarette, offers me the pack, and I take one. I finished my pack already and didn't feel like going back to my room for more.

"Point." I let him light my cigarette. "Anyway there's only so many of these parties are gonna happen before something goes south. Maybe it's a miracle that we even had one good one."

"Probably." Gotta hand it to Butler, he has the good sense not to give empty reassurances. Or contradict me for the sake of it. Maybe he feels it too, that sense that while nothing's *wrong* yet, maybe, it isn't right either.

He walks with me, and as we pass the pool, which has some early-morning sunbathers in bikinis with their mimosas, I hear one of them say "Did you notice one of the robot dogs is wearing a bow?" and I manage to not laugh my head off and make it so we have to interact or something.

Most of Bristol's party people are not early risers, though, like I know for a fact that we won't see Marquis before noon and that might even be noon Eastern Standard Time, so when we see her and Will inside, they're alone. "Still enjoying the honeymoon period?" I ask, and Will flushes and Bristol smiles tightly.

"Actually, Dolly, I'm going to need your help with something before this evening's festivities, if you wouldn't mind."

"Mind? I'd be honored," I say, thinking it's a mistake that I don't ask 'help with what' but also I guess I can still say no later.

"Perfect, darling, thank you. Around six, say?"

"Oh, we're havin' an early bird party tonight?"

"I'm making an effort to strike the balance between our night owls and early risers," she says. She tilts her head just slightly, looking at me critically. "Must you always carry that gun?"

"It's almost like you forgot what's goin' on, Bristles, did you get a knock in the head that I forgot about?"

Her smile doesn't falter, but her eyes sharpen a little. "It's making my guests uncomfortable."

"Now, that's a thing to choose to lie about," I say, grinning hard, keeping our eye contact but in my periphery, I see Will react just slightly. He's a fast learner, he remembers what me and Bitsy said yesterday. "Not a single one of them has the sense to know what they're looking for, and if I'm making them uncomfortable, that's just by merit of my scintillatin' personality."

Butler has the good sense to stay out of this, and so does Will, and I watch Bristol run her social calculation which is not normally something you really see behind the curtain on, and it only takes a split second and her smile changes, apologetic now. "You're right, darling, I'm so sorry. What a silly thing for me to do, after all we've been through together. Can you just forget I said anything?"

"Sure," I say easily. "We're all under a lot of pressure." I wink at Will. "Anyway, at least one guest knows I'm strapped." I literally just mentioned a double cross, but I was talking about Will, not Bristol. It never occurred to me to worry about Bristol. Should I be?

"Splendid, thank you. I'll see you at six, then." They split off and go off towards the pool.

"Gonna go talk to Bits," I say to Butler, and leave him to go find her.

———————————

"I don't know when she would've had the chance to talk to anybody," Bits says carefully. "I don't *think* Bristol would want to double cross us. It doesn't make sense."

"No, it doesn't. But I wanted to actually say it and have you tell me that." I take a deep breath, let it out. "I'm not used to things like 'the strain getting to me.'" I make elaborate air quotes to get her to laugh.

"The price of giving up your cybernetic supersoldier programming, I assume," she says.

"We did that *ages* ago."

"Yeah, and have had various stress levels since, but I think not this kind of sustained level of anticipatory stress."

"Keep talkin' sense to me, Bitsy, we might be getting somewhere." We're in the same room where she was deprogramming Will. Wonder how many more people Bits will get to deprogram; two already is kind of a lot. I should ask Butler how he got his done; is it weird that we haven't already talked about it? I know he has, though. He doesn't whistle anymore.

"It makes sense to be jumpy, and it makes sense for you to double check your impulses. Nothing you're doing is wrong." She's got her headset pushed up on top of her head, her hair going every which way. "There has been a lot of chatter on the agency network today. If we hadn't done such a good job undermining Will's credibility, we'd be in trouble already."

"It's nice of you to say 'we' when you're the one who did all the heavy lifting."

"We got here as a team," she says, reaching for her glass of coffee. I look at the pitcher on the table; the same jet fuel, I think. I chew on my lip instead of saying anything, she's a grown up.

"But also I think they've got people on the way, if some aren't here already. They're being very circumspect."

"I ever tell you that in the program, they put us in VR and tested our precognitive abilities."

She raises her eyebrows at me, but finishes drinking first. "No, you never talked about it."

She read my file from front to back, of course. I know that, she knows that. "I was awful at it. But there was *one* time I was sure about the test thing and I was right." She blinks at me. "I guess it was bound to happen sooner or later, with enough repetitions of the test."

"Some of the program separated off the people with what they thought were demonstrative precognitive abilities," Bits says. "With you, the notes said that you're able to rapidly put together context clues, which sometimes makes it seem as though you've had a precursor indicator but really you're just very good at subconsciously reacting to the environment."

"Well we knew that." I mean, I didn't, when I was a wet-behind-the-ears kid in a cybernetic supersoldier program, but we sure as hell know that by now.

"Sure, but we can really leverage it at times like this." She frowns. "I mean, in theory. Not like I know how to turn *up* your situational awareness."

"More's the pity." I wonder if the program that trained pre-cognitives kept going somewhere, or if it got mothballed too.Wouldn't that be funny, if they were still operating some-where, givin' world governments a nudge here and there. "Anyway, I hope the real action kicks off soon, before I end up putting one of Bristol's guests against a wall."

"Are you worried that you'll do that?"

"Not really, but this many fancy people around, there's no telling what can happen."

"Maybe you should do some more laps. Or go in the ocean, did you do that yet?"

"Maybe that's a good idea. Get some beach time in before six."

Her eyes move to the side, I guess checking an AR calendar. "What's at six?"

"I dunno, Bristol asked me to help her with something then."

"Dinner's at seven, according to the kitchen calendar."

"Well who knows, maybe she wanted to get me alone for some reason." I wiggle my eyebrows at Bits, who frowns first and then laughs.

"I'm sure."

Chapter Eight

Going out to the actual beach and into the little waves does actually do me some good, I think. Everybody has the good sense to leave me alone, even Butler, and none of the party people come out to the beach when there's a perfectly good pool right there. They've got music playing, not too loud, and sometimes voices get raised loud enough that I can kind of hear their echo, but they're not particularly *rowdy* party people. I've seen worse, and I'm not even talking about my military experience.

I rinse off and throw clothes on and get to Bristol's door at six sharp. She's wearing yet another one of those silky, gauzy robe things when she answers, and her hair and makeup are already done. I think. They look done, anyway. "What's up?" I ask, and she all but pulls me inside.

"This is going to be such fun, you'll see," she says, her eyes actually twinkling.

"Bristles, your idea of fun and mine don't have a lotta overlap."

"Mmm, true," she says, shutting the door and then bringing me into her room's little living room. I guess it's a suite, that she's got. There's a hassock or footstool or whatever in the middle of the room, and a couple of spray cans on the coffee table.

"Is this something you could've asked Marquis for?" I ask, and then realize I only saw Marquis last night, and only for a little while. Not today.

"Oh, Marquis was called away to Paris, to assess the legitimacy of a painting."

"I didn't realize Marquis did stuff like that." The cans look like too-tall spray paint cans and I can't see any writing on them from my angle.

"They have degrees in museum studies and have worked in galleries and facilities all over the world," Bristol says. "And so it falls to you, as Bits isn't tall enough and Will would not be appropriate to ask."

"Suzette?" This is making me weirdly nervous and I don't know why. Maybe because she hasn't said yet what the help is.

"Busy with her own outfit for tonight. Really, darling, it's quite simple, you—"

"Bristol, how am I gonna be *outfit* help?"

"Honestly, Dolly." She picks up one of the spray cans, which rattles, and hands it to me. "I'm going to stand on this stool and you're going to go around me and spray my dress on, and I'll adjust as necessary. I want you to walk around so that it'll drape like fabric cut on the bias."

"Spray your dress on." I turn the can over in my hands. It says, essentially, "dress in a can" in French. A designer name, I assume, and an ingredients list. Silk fibers, synthetic, suspended in stuff I don't really have the vocabulary for because they aren't food words or violence words.

"Yes, so you understand now?"

"I guess. At least you've got more'n one, for if I fuck it up."

"You won't, I'm confident you'll do fine." She picks up her phone and shows me a picture, like I'm gonna be able to spray a dress on her that looks like that. "Just start behind me, on my right shoulder, and like I said..."

"Yeah," I say, squinting at the picture and rattling the can. She pushes the phone in my hand and drops her robe, stepping up onto the stool. I pop the cap and look from the picture to her and stop again. "*No* dragonscale, Bristles?"

"I simply cannot be armored at all times, Dolly, it's impossible." She looks over her shoulder at me. "Besides, it isn't as though *you* did either, when you were swimming this afternoon? Be reasonable."

"Fair enough." I guess the camisole or whatever would ruin the lines of the spray dress the way bra and underwear don't. What do I know.

"Oh it's cold," she says when I start spraying, a laugh in her voice, her skin rippling gooseflesh.

"Should I stop?" Watching the spray turn into fabric is wild, like magic. It's white; it's interesting how often Bristol wears white. Just strikes me as impractical.

"No, no, it'll be fine." There's a mirror across from her, of course, and a door to the secret passages behind it. She watches the fabric form in the mirror, making adjustments a couple of times, and I do my best to concentrate. I'm not an uncontrollable horndog, but Bristol's charms cannot be overstated. We've gotta work together, I made the decision a long time ago not to even try to pursue.

The can is starting to sputter when I'm at the hem and I say, "I guess that's it."

She's looking at herself in the mirror, critically, and looks down at the skirt. "Do you have a knife?"

"Yeah." I pull a folding jackknife and a combat knife and hold them both out to her. She rolls her eyes, but she's smiling just a little, and she actually picks the combat knife and traces a slit up the skirt.

"Hold that taut?" I do, and she makes the actual cut, and the fabric pulls apart and then the edges roll over and sorta heal themselves instead of fraying. She hands the knife back and then fiddles with the straps, pulling them out a little bit and laying them down so it's more off the shoulder. "How is the back?"

I clear my throat. "I'm not exactly a neutral audience," I say. Our eyes meet in the mirror.

"Thank you for your help, darling, I don't know what I would've done without you," she says, stepping down and going over to her jewelry table. Her sandals stand at ready over there too.

"No problem," I say, stowing my knives again. "I'll see you later." For a second I think about how funny it would be to exit via secret passage, without saying anything, but I take the door instead. I go back out onto the beach, drop my clothes in the sand, and dive into the surf again.

─────────────

When I get out of the shower, Butler's in my room. "What's up?" I call, toweling off.

"How'd you know I was here?"

"Smelled your cologne." Is that how, or is that my flash-in-the-pan precognitive abilities. I look at the mirror, and a heart drawn there in the steam makes me smile. Guess he must've done that last night. "Where've you been?"

"Talking to Will."

"What, really?" I pull the bathroom door open, sloppily wrapped in a towel. The towels here, or in my room anyway, aren't the terrycloth loop kind, and I feel like they don't actually get me dry, just kinda slick the water around. He's sitting on the foot of the bed. "About what?"

"We're both in love with difficult women." He pats what he can reach as I go past.

"Isn't everybody? What, you got a club?" I grin at him and rummage in my clothes. I should do laundry at some point, before we're likely to start bleedin'.

"It's part of what we were hashing out, bylaws and shit."

"We've all been spending too much time *talking*," I say, throwing my towel at him and wrestling into my clothes. "At this point I'd rather somebody just shot at us."

"That bad, huh?"

"Asshole." I sit next to him to put my boots on. "Sorry."

He puts an arm around me and kisses the top of my head. "It's fine. I'd rather you go swimming than go lookin' for hallucinogenic tequila," he murmurs against my hair.

"You don't really get a say." I stay leaning into him for a little while, though. He always smells good.

"I know." He kisses me again, then lets me go and I finish putting my boots on. "Waiting isn't good for anybody and they're probably doing it on purpose."

"It's possible we're already fucked, honestly, but we gotta just find that out for ourselves."

"That's more like it." He laughs. "Anyway, it's also giving me time to train the kids."

"With Will?"

"He's a good shot, and steady enough when you aren't around."
I laugh. "No, really."

"No, I believe you. And can't help but think how smart it is that
you're tricking him into making connections with people here
other'n Bristol."

"Don't know if I'm tricking him," Butler says with a shrug. "Anyway, he seems comfortable enough with Bits."

"Bits isn't the kind of existential threat that makes him nervous."
I flop back on the bed. "How's it going with the kids, though?
Tell me. Should I be helping?"

"It's okay to do what you're doing," he says. "They're taking it seriously, which is more than I can say about us when we started."

"Excuse yourself, I took it very seriously."

"Sure you did." He lays next to me, props himself on an elbow.
"You've always wanted to make sure the big dogs know you're a
big dog too."

I move my gaze from the ceiling to his face. "Well I am."

"I always knew it."

And he always acted like it, too. "Sorry I lost my belt buckle," I
say after a few minutes. He looks surprised and his eyes drop to
my belt. Then he smiles, leans down and kisses me.

"It's just stuff. We'll go back to the old swimming hole sometime and you can find another piece of something to use. For the next one."

The party is the same. The robot dogs patrol outside of the lights, Marge and Floyd and Joker and Butler and I hover around at the edges of things, very occasionally engaging with Bristol's guests. I watch Nicolai and Suzette make eye contact from across the room and little by little get closer to each other as the night progresses, until finally he makes the first move, snagging two glasses of champagne off a tray and going to offer her one. I'm sure they'll make beautiful babies. Or, have a torrid, no-strings affair and come away from their time here having made a new hookup friend. Whichever. Something good coming out of this mess. In theory, more good'll come out of this, but we gotta get there. It's not like the agency's been persistently causing us *that* much trouble. Actually, it's kinda funny how little overall impact they've had on us.

I didn't get to see Will's face when he first saw Bristol in that dress, but just like last night, she keeps him near her most of the time, and I do see the glances he keeps giving her. Suzette's outfit doesn't look like anything special to me, but who knows, maybe she had to iron it or something.

//I think we're okay tonight// Bits messages me at one point. //Airport and actual ports are quiet, agency chatter is about normal level. If they're smart, they'll fly in somewhere else and drive over.//

"If you say so," I say.

//You sound disappointed.//

"Bored. Anticipation fatigue."

//I get it.// Bits knows better than to tell me to try and enjoy the party. //How are Floyd and Joker?//

"They've got the basics. They've seen zero action, so who knows how that'd shake out. But they've been okay for this, they're eager to please, and Marge is good. Plus, Butler and Will have been working with them. Both to save our hides and also for something to do." One of the robot dogs trundles past me; Mr. Squeak, it's got the bow. And an empty can of Power Horse on its back. "Have the dog patrols ever noticed anything weird?"

//Like recently, or in the history of ever?// A pause, and I wait, because I know she's checking. //Yeah, the Loki designate tased somebody three months ago and they ran off before Marge could get to them. Mr. Squeak, no, and Snorri had somebody put a bikini bottom on it just this afternoon. Yes, I cross checked the cameras, it was one of the invited guests.//

"I don't know if I should say poor Snorri or lucky Snorri."

//Dealer's choice.//

I laugh, and one of the guests walking by carrying her heels looks at me and I wink. She giggles uncertainly and keeps walking. She's the Crayola heiress or something, I'm sure. I saw an invite list, Marge had it, but I didn't exactly commit it to memory.

None of these people interest me, other than threat mitigation. "Hey, is Marquis really in Paris?"

Another pause, I assume while Bits recalibrates. //Yeah. Why?//

"It seemed like they left awfully soon."

//They got the call this morning.// I hear Bristol laugh, and from where I'm standing can just get a glimpse of her on Will's arm, but not who she's talking to. //We can't do this. Second guessing each other.// I can imagine the look of careful concern on Bits's face.

"No, it's bad for business." But then, so is going to your private hotel and filling it with a rotating cast of mostly-strangers right after stealing some kinda double-hush government agent. "Plus, it's good for Marquis not to have more contact with the agency. They got when the gettin' was good the first time around."

//That might've contributed to their early departure.//

"Makes sense. Plus Paris is like, right there." It is and it isn't. Everything's closer together here than stateside, anyway. "It'd be better for the agency if they didn't have more contact with us, too."

//I'm sure they don't see it that way, that's not how government agencies work.//

"Yeah, I know. But it'd be nice, right?" Wishing it wasn't going like this won't change anything, but if wishes were horses then beggars could ride.

Chapter Nine

W hen things go wrong, it's so quick and clean that we almost don't realize at first. We're tipped off pretty quick,
but that's a combination of one robot dog going dark, Mr.
Squeak tasing somebody, and Bristol hitting her panic button. I
almost get to her in time. Bristol hits that button and Bits shows
me a blip of where on property she is, and I take the shortest way
to it. Of course they hear me coming. I'm not careful. I don't
think about like. Stealth.

I get a glimpse of Bristol's face and the flip of her skirt, disap-
pearing around a corner, as I come out of one of this place's long
dark hallways and something, somebody, hits me in the middle
of the chest and slams me to the ground on my back. I hear a
sound that I know is my head hitting those nice shiny tiles but
I put that away for later, I'm hyped up enough I can do that. I
kip up onto my feet, slapping for my knife, because everything is
still so fucking *quiet,* I don't want to bring gunplay into this just
yet. I still think that I can stop them here.

I tag the guy twice in a stab vest and then once for real, I feel
it land and hear him grunt, and then he catches my wrist and
gives a yank and a twist, meant to disarm me, which it does, and
break my arm, which it doesn't, because it's my cybernetic arm.
I see his face then; it's Clancy, the pile of muscle they had doing security when we ran that diamond job where we all got so
cozy. Guys like that really take it to heart when you make 'em

look bad, and it's on me that he surprised me. I'm running those thoughts in my brain separate of all my combat-reaction-space; times like these, I understand Bitsy's data deluge.

He's still got my arm and doesn't much like it when I head butt him but he isn't letting *go* and I grab on with my other hand and let him hold me up while I plant both boots in his stomach-ribs-crotch area. He lets me go then, because he throws me, and I clip off the corner at the end of the hallway, my air woofing out, and thump on the floor again, curled around my poor ribs. I use the wall to drag myself to my feet, and he smirks, and then the wind of a suppressed round passes over my shoulder. He isn't hit, but he puts a finger to his ear in classic comms pose and then goes off the way I saw Bristol get taken.

I take a step to follow and stagger instead, catching the wall again, getting that next breath finally. My head's trying to spin and I can't tell yet what's happening in my ribs and back. "Woah hey, Dolly, hey," Butler says, holstering his handgun, stopping short of touching me. I know that gentled-down tone of voice he's using. Haven't heard it in a while but I've heard it a lot. "Stop, take it easy."

"No, they went—"

//They're offsite// Bits says. //Time to regroup.//

"Dolly, look at me." Butler's in front of me, trying to catch my gaze as I'm bending to pick up my knife. I wipe my nose with the back of my hand, blink at the blood. I'm pretty tired of breaking my nose, actually. Wonder if I can get a cybernetic replacement. I laugh, and Butler frowns. "How many fingers?"

"You know that doesn't happen with us, they fixed that," I say, brushing his hand away. I forget what part of the permanent supersoldier suite negates, or tries like hell to negate, concussions. I cracked my head bad enough for one, whatever, no arguments there. But for us it doesn't mean anything. "We gotta go get the one they left and see what we can get out of him."

"Sure, but—" While we're standing there wasting time, one of the little mopping robots whirrs out and starts cleaning blood off the tiles. Mine or Clancy's, I can't bother about it right now.

"Please, Butler." He shuts his mouth and we go. He watches me, but I can breathe and I can walk.

Snorri is the robot dog that went dark, and that's just because it got a sport coat thrown over it, and Marge has to get Loki to stand down, because it went and covered Will once the other robot dogs activated. Part of the special other programming that Bits did without really laying out in detail for the rest of the class. I listen to that chatter as Butler gets the agent zip tied and drags him by the tuxedo collar to a nearby non-guest-occupied room to further secure him to a straight backed chair. I pull the curtain tiebacks off their hooks and let my hands remember the right kind of knot.

We, well mostly Butler, give him a quick patdown, take his handgun and take a keycard that he's got tucked into his shirt pocket. How the party's still going, I don't know. It started even earlier today, four instead of six, or maybe it never really ended last night, just some people went to bed and other people didn't and it's like partying by shift work.

Marge brings Will in while I'm still deciding if I want to wait and hear what this guy has to say, or if I'm gonna just break his neck and go get Bristol, no matter the sidelong looks Butler's giving me. Loki clatters in behind them, which is fine, but what I really want is for Bits to get in here.

"Shit, I'm sorry," Marge says. "I did what I could but—"

"We all did, and it wasn't enough. The kids okay?" I know they are but I gotta get her refocused.

"Yeah, they checked in, they're fine. Didn't see anything either. The guests are still happy."

"That's fine. Don't feel bad, and don't let 'em feel bad. Just you three do business as usual, this is very much above your pay grade." I remember how to put a smile on. "It's why the whole gang is here."

She looks at my face, looks at the guy in the chair. Looks at Butler. She wants to protest, she wants to help, and I just need her out of my way. It isn't that I can't trust her, it's that we need to keep the party going, keep up appearances, and get this fixed behind the scenes. Bristol's got too many people here from too many walks of life for them to know that anything just went down. "Understood," she finally says. "You tell me if you need me for anything."

"Thanks Marge. Really, it's appreciated." She stalks off, leaving Loki, and the second she's out of earshot, I whip around and chokeslam Will up against the nearest wall. "Did you know this was going to happen?".

He, well, he can't answer and I let up just enough. I know my own strength, I know what I'm doing. "I thought they would come for *me*," he says, in a gasp.

"Did they decide they want her instead or is she bait?"

"I don't know, I have no way to know." I think about choking him again, he's always expected me to hurt him, and I drop him instead. The guy in the chair hasn't come around yet so either he's faking or Mr. Squeak got him worse than a normal taser and we're wasting *time* and then Bits comes in, with Nicolai, and I'm glad to see that. Nicolai's good to have at your back.

"What're we lookin' at, Bitsy?" I wipe my nose again. Bleeding stopped.

"They want to trade."

"How do you know that already?" Will's still backed up against the wall and I'm still way too close to him for his comfort, but I turn to her. Her expression doesn't tend to give away much in the best of times, and right now ain't exactly the best of times. Them taking Bristol, out of all of us, is the worst thing they could do to her, after everything. And they *know* it.

"They called Will's phone."

"And you talked to them?" That's not the question I mean. I hard blink to refocus. "What did they say?"

She'd been starting to answer, stops, blinks. "I answered, and they said to bring Will to an address, and texted that address. It's a hotel by the airport, pretty touristy and busy. They don't have it emptied, that I can tell, from records and street and security cameras."

"They're assuming collateral will protect them." The guy in the chair makes kind of a snoring noise, then snorts and the chair creaks, so I guess he's awake now. "Hello sunshine," I say. He looks around the room, looks up at Butler, then looks over at me, and at Will. He tries to get up, realizes he's attached to the chair he's in, *and* zip tied, and sets his jaw.

"I don't know what you think you'll—"

"We don't really need you, I just kept you for funsies," I say. "Did they even mention this guy, Bitsy?"

"No," she says. If the guy was going to say anything else right then, that shut him up. I wonder if he's got any comms equipment on him, but if he does, that's Bitsy's territory. My territory right now is getting Bristol back.

"Will, what's the play here?" I step back, give him some breathing room.

"What? I—" He looks at my face, gathers himself. "We...the agency hasn't had to deal with this particular situation before. I assume the goal is asset recovery. And/or damage control."

"Bits, gimme his phone, and an alternate address."

"What kind of alternate address?" She hands me the phone, slowly, frowning.

"It can still be populated, if that's what you mean. We want them to think that we're changing addresses to assert a sense of control over the situation." It'll also mean making Bristol go through getting moved more'n once but maybe they're just in a holding pattern driving her around town right now. Actually. "Where *is* Bristol?"

She pauses, looking. "In a car, moving. Sort of towards the hotel, but like they're taking the long way?"

Oh this is fun isn't it. "Pick a mall or something. A market." The guy tied to the chair takes a breath like he's gonna say something. "Will, can you put the fear of God in him, I ain't exactly got the time right now."

"Um," Will says, and I can't help but laugh, which has an ugly edge to it, all things considered.

"Do you even know each other? Are you *colleagues*?" I ask.

"We've met," Will says stiffly. Oh he's feeling his deprogramming now. I wonder if he doesn't even know the secret handshake anymore. That's gonna fuck him when we hand him over. Guess he's probably already fucked.

"Well you've met, and you're the only agent who takes us seriously, so make him understand that I will kill him and not care. You get that, right?"

"I get that," Will says. The other agent is listening silently, resentfully.

"Actually, wait, you. What's your name?" He looks at me. "Nevermind I don't care. Tell me what your plan was." Still silent. "What was the *operation*."

"Why would I tell you?" Welp.

"So I don't break every bone you got." I get behind him and start with his pinkie, that one's easy and won't really mess up his life too much. If he lives through this. If you've never had somebody break one of your bones on purpose, it's a very unpleasant surprise, both how easy it can be and just how much it hurts. Bones aren't typically brittle or dry, so if you've ever tried to break a green stick of wood, you know how there's a *flex* first, it's got *give*. It bends before it breaks. When it's flexing, he's doing a clean inhale through his nostrils; maybe he's broken a bone before. When it goes, though, he lets out a guttural noise. I'm watching Will as I do it, and he's got on a brave face but I'm not so sure how his stomach is, and there's a way he flinches around the eyes. "Hope you're not right handed." I move in to his ring finger, and as it's flexing, he says,

"The op was to extract Will Scarlet, but we had a timer. If it was getting too close to time and he couldn't be extracted, one of you three was the next option. If that was also unattainable, then we were to pull out. No wetworks."

And try again for another party. God damn it. "There, see how easy that was?" I wink at Will and let go of the guy's hand. "Remind me to rough you up a little before all this is done, so they can't tell you caved immediately. If you think your devices're recording, no they aren't." He must've looked at Will, who nods. "So they always wanted you back, Will Scarlet, ain't that sweet." Or they want to kill him themselves. That seems likely.

Nicolai rattles ice in a drink, reminding me about the rest of us in the room. Tunnel vision sure is a thing. "Dolly, what is the play?"

"We get Bristol back, obviously. And she's the one who wanted Will, no offense Will, so I don't really give a shit what happens to him." She isn't a helpless maiden, maybe she stabbed one of 'em and then took out the driver and is on her way back here on her own. She'll come clacking in, her hair down around her shoulders, and laugh at us for worrying. I look at the door. She doesn't do that.

"No offense taken," he says carefully. "I agree with that plan."

"Good, super simple." I glance around the room. Butler and Nicolai each have a drink and are just waiting for me to call the shots, good. Except Butler's watching me like he wants to bench me and he can't do that. I guess he's the closest to somebody I'd listen to, but we don't have that luxury and I'm not so bad off. Mildly concussed, a couple cracked and or bruised parts, mostly ribs, I'll sort it out later. Chew some excedrin. Bits has that far-away look on her face that means she's tracking more data than I can even conceive of; maybe listenin' on Bristol's devices while looking at agency chatter. Seems like a good guess. "Ready for me to make this call, Bitsy? Picked a place?"

"I picked a place. There's supposed to be an open-air market by a French import shop. Kind of open, not really crowded right now but not no public, good approach and egress vectors."

"Good, so we can put Butler and Nicolai up with rifles."

"Maybe deploy a robot dog," Butler says. "Keep them from circling in on us with more personnel."

"Never thought I'd hear you say that," I say. "That's what we call growth. Yeah we'll give Snorri the chance to get payback."

Butler sighs, just slightly, and finishes his whiskey. The picture of calm control. "I forgot you named them."

"They're good names." I redial the number that called Will's phone last. It rings six times and I assume the call will dump and then Harding says, "I assume this isn't Will."

"Got it in one," I say.

"Is there a problem with the arrangement?"

"Yeah, we're changin' the venue. Hopefully you can accommodate that. As Bristol would say."

"The ever-charming Bristol," he says, in that combination of frustration and admiration I know well from every other god-damn person in the world who has ever had to deal with Bristol as anything but the party girl. He wants me to be mad, though, he wants me to react, and I wait. I think about lighting a cigarette but don't. I could use a cigarette. I could use non-broken ribs. "Of course we can accommodate a change of venue, if you're amenable to the rest of the agreement."

"Yeah I don't give a fuck about Will, you can have him back. In one piece, even."

"That's very nice to know. I don't suppose I can speak to Will."

"I don't suppose I can speak to Bristol?" A pause. "I figured. So yeah, not at this time." I hope to Christ they didn't drug her.

"Understandable." There's a pause, where he muffles the phone. "I don't suppose you've seen another of our misplaced agents?"

"We only stole the one," I say. "But if you can describe the agent, we'll keep an eye out. As a professional courtesy."

"Noted. Maybe we'll belay that for now, since we're so chummy."

"Suit yourself." Interesting that the agent, who is not gagged or anything, is also not trying to communicate when I'm on the phone. Guess he's a quick learner. "Okay, so by the French import shop, there's an open air market. I figure that'll do us."

"Is that so." He's deciding if he wants to fuck with us more and we both know it. He's deciding if it's worth it, and I hope for his sake and the sake of the two agents in the room with me that he makes the right decision. "We can make that happen. See you in an hour?"

"An hour sounds good, roger that."

"I'm glad you're being reasonable, Dolly. There's no reason this can't go smoothly."

"Agreed, Harding. You're a real sport." He hangs up. "He never described you," I say to the other agent. "Didn't know you were on his shit list, huh?" The guy doesn't say anything, just stares at me sullenly. "Oh, don't pout, I might start crackin' fingers again to see if there's anything else interesting you might have to tell me, like how many of you were on site tonight and how many're in town total. We know you've got a small operation. Did you come here in the sub?"

"The sub is mothballed," Will says.

"Aw, that's a shame. We all liked the sub, right Bitsy?" She pulled on her headset at some point, and kind of makes a noise at me that might be an assent.

The other agent doesn't say anything, and I shrug and go back to his fingers. I get to the pointer before he grates out, "Four of us came to the party. Ten total came to Morocco. Plus Harding." The pain of betrayal doesn't stand up to the pain of broken fingers, I guess. They used to build 'em stronger. Or I shouldn't have made fun of how easy he cracked the first time.

"Atta boy, thanks." So ten left. Could be a hundred and could be just Harding, for all it matters, if we play nice when we trade. They wouldn't do all this if they were just gonna frag Will and dump him in the desert. In theory. I don't fucking know. "Anyway, Butler, Nicky, get goin' and we'll see you on the other side. Bits'll give you the location if she hasn't already, and cut surveillance for you to get in position, if she hasn't already." Guess we're solidly in "what Dolly wants to do" territory, sorry Bristol is missing it.

"I'm sorry about all this," Will says, maybe to keep me from breaking his fingers too. Maybe he is actually sorry about all this. Sorry for Bristol, anyway.

"Sure you are," I say. "Butler, you really gonna take one of the robot dogs?"

"Might as well. Or two. Like I said, be nice to have something watching our backs when you're doing the heavy lifting." He gives me a long look.

"I can drive a car and do a handoff," I say. More true than guessing at how okay I feel.

"Okay."

"What about him, though?" Nicolai asks, not exactly *nervous* but not really comfortable with letting it go either. We all look at the agent in the chair.

"Good question," I say. He's extraneous, he doesn't have anything to do with the leverage or negotiations, he just got his ass tased by a robot dog and we found him before he got himself together enough to leave again. "He's not really worth anything to us."

"Meaning?" I close my eyes a second, feel the world try to spin, and then look at Butler.

"I guess blindfold him and leave him in an alley someplace and they'll pick him up after this is done." Nicky looks dubious and Butler looks surprised. "Look, you got a better idea, go for it. We wanna zero out the ledgers here." I dunno if that's exactly the saying I mean, but it gets the point across. What's a few broken fingers amongst uneasy truce-holders?

"Okay then. Looks like you're coming with us," Butler says, and pulls the knot I used; my hands remember, his hands remember.

"I don't—" the guy starts to say, and Butler give him a shake, like a dog with a rope.

"Trust me, you want to get away from her. And your agency'll pick you up. This is a good outcome for you." The agent doesn't say anything else.

Chapter Ten

═══

W e get to the meetup, Bits using her active camo in the back seat, so it looks like it's just me and Will. The other end of the market, Harding comes out of a car, alone, which makes me check rooftops. //Clear// Bits says in my ear. //No idea why. Butler and Nicolai didn't run into anybody to clean up.//

"Is it possible they're *actually* just doing a clean handoff?" I ask Bitsy but also for Will's benefit. I don't ask where they dropped off the other agent. Maybe a hospital, what a courtesy that'd be.

"Maybe?" Will says. It's interesting how calm he is, actually, commendable. Maybe he still trusts the government. Wonder what that's like; even when I was in the program, it wasn't the government I trusted. It was the people I knew that were also in the program. It was the promise that we'd all come out the other side better off.

//Loki's giving the all clear too. And Snorri. Well. Snorri scared a stray cat or something but then it was all clear.//

"Reassuring." I look at Will. "Okay, you ready? Any last words?"

"I don't think that's necessary," he says.

"Suit yourself." In a movie, I'd be checking my handgun again before getting out of the car, but I already did that back at the hotel, this isn't a movie, I get out of the car and raise my hand to Harding. Wonder what, if anything, Clancy told him about our meeting.

There are people here, going about their lives, browsing the market, whatever, but after a moment he sees me and nods, goes around to the passenger side of the car and opens the door to hand Bristol out. They start walking our way, which is, I think, a real show of good faith on his part.

//Target acquired// Butler says in my ear. //Let me know if you need me to take the shot.//

"Understood," I say, and go open Will's door, though he's been a very good boy and not required any kind of extra handling. Really, we picked him at just the right time, plus the deprogramming. I don't look at Bits, don't look back at the car as we start walking to meet Harding and Bristol, and neither does Will. Am I starting to feel bad about this? Shit.

Bristol's face changes a little when she sees that it's just me and Will, the mask slipping for a heartbeat. She returns to her serene neutral expression almost immediately, but I wonder what she hoped for. I wonder what she thought we were doing. When we're close enough, she breaks loose of Harding's hand on her arm or he lets her go, and she flings herself into Will's arms. He looks at me over the top of her head, and I can see that conflict there too, in his wide eyes, that question too. What did she think this was. What don't we know, that she does. They didn't drug her, though, her movements are normal, her eyes, when I saw them, were clear.

I could give Butler the signal, but this is too open, and then there'd still be nine agents left, and we'd have to Whac-a-Mole back to the hotel and even then, what? Have Floyd and Joker and Marge pick them off? Plus local law enforcement. No, if the agency's playing nice we have to play nice, there are too many civilians here.

"Well, Mr. Harding, I wish I could say it was a pleasure," I say. He's also watching the embrace, and I also can't read the look on his face.

"In another life," he says, maybe poetically, maybe regretfully. I can only assume he's read my file by now, or a file about the program, such as Bits left available for him. Probably that's part of what she's doing in the car right now, erasing us. Erasing this. She spends so much time erasing us. Maybe at some point, Harding had visions of what it would be like, to bring us over. Maybe that's why he entertained the notion of extracting us.

Will turns to me, his arm still around Bristol's shoulders. "Dolly, get her out of here."

"Sure thing," I say, because yeah that's the plan, and at the same time Bristol says,

"Absolutely not, what could you possibly mean?"

"Please, Dolly," he says, as she's twisting to look up into his face.

"Will, *no*, I'm not some damsel to be handed off and *protected*. We'll—"

But I see what's in his face, and I understand, or think I understand. He's got a plan too, and he made it with Bits, I assume. Or I hope to Christ he made it with Bits at least, maybe Butler and Nicolai too, and they didn't tell Bristol and they didn't tell me, because they needed this to be real. And because he knows I love her too.

"Yeah, we're going," I say, and Bristol whips around to me.

"*Dolly*." She's furious, she's heartbroken, and I take her by the arm, gently, and she tears her arm out of my grasp and dodges back a few steps as I grab for her again. "Dolly, we are *not* letting him do this!" This is the first time I've ever heard her voice break. I see at least one glance from shoppers, but everybody is very determined to mind their business this time of night and in public.

"Bristol. Come on." Bristol does not come on. Will shifts behind her, getting nervous, needing us gone. He's got a sense of a timer that I've only just become aware of. If they did this while I spent all that time being bored, it'll be worth it. If we can pull it off. If he lives through it. If we all live through it. "Bristol, I don't wanna hurt you."

Bristol lowers her voice, her eyes electric. "Dolly, if you do this, I will never forgive you."

"I'd rather you be alive than forgive me," I say, and she turns around to Will, to do I don't know what, and I grab her around the waist and haul her off, and she *yells* at me, the prim and proper princess yells and struggles and she's always been stronger than she looks, but not strong enough. I grit my teeth and acknowledge and then ignore the pain in my ribs, shoving her into the car. She tries to open the door again the second I close it but Bits keeps that door locked. Nobody tries to stop us, but there is distinctly less crowd now, people filtering out of the thoroughfare.

I slide across the hood and get behind the wheel, even as Will and Harding are walking back to Harding's car, and Butler and Nicolai cover as we get out of there and drive to Bristol's hotel. It would make sense to do it in a circuitous way, but they've known where we were the whole time. So I don't do that. She stops trying to jump out, once we're moving. Buckles her belt, even. She pulls out her phone but then throws it on the dashboard in disgust, Bitsy coming through once again.

The parking lot is still full, and the party music is still floating out of the windows, up from the back patio. I park, and turn to her to say something about cleaning up and getting back to it, distracted by whatever my back is doing, and she shocks me by slapping me full across the face, hard enough that my eyes water.

"How *could* you?" The world is see-sawing and I can't see her face. My friggin' *nose*.

"Bristol, I—" She slaps me again, putting her all into it, and I manage to catch her wrist before she connects on the third one. She twists away and gets out of the car, slamming the door. She never acts like this, never. She must really think they're gonna hurt him. Like, worse than a mindwipe agent reset. Or she thinks they're gonna kill him. But also she'd be horrified if anybody saw her like this. I get out of the car, lean on the roof, and call to her in my best 'everything is normal' tone, "Bristles, come on. Party's still going." She stops, her back to me, completely rigid, and I watch her flex her hands. Then I watch her give her head a little toss, and I can imagine her pulling the composure back over her face, her whole self. Somehow, she doesn't have a single hair askew, I didn't notice that before now. And then she goes back inside to her party, the rhythm of her high heels steady and normal on the tiles.

Bits gets out of the car next to me, her VR headset hung around her neck, blinking against the now-setting sun. "Sorry," she says

"Tell me there's a plan," I say, once I don't have to lean on the car anymore, getting out my pack of cigarettes and lighting one.

"There's a plan." She rummages through her pockets, comes out with a battered, rattling pill bottle, and she shakes out a couple to hand me.

I exhale the first lungful of smoke. "Thanks." I dry swallow them without even checking what they are, drag on my cigarette again. "You need me?"

"I will." She's looking at me, really looking, and I avoid her eyes. Think about how I'm breathing. "You're—"

"Everybody keeps asking if I'm okay, and somebody's not gonna be."

She gives a nod, looks at her phone. "When Butler and Nicolai get back."

"Understood." Bits goes inside too, leaving me alone with my thoughts, which was kinda the opposite of what I wanted but that's life I guess. I'm gonna have to apologize to her for that. It wasn't too bad, but also is probably the worst thing I've ever said to Bits.

I'm sitting on the hood of the car, my boots on the bumper and elbows on my knees, up to my third cigarette when Butler and Nicolai park next to me. It's a position that doesn't so much hurt, gargoyled over like that. Butler cuts the engine and then pops the trunk, and the robot dogs climb out and skitter back into the hotel. Even without faces I can tell Snorri from Loki and I'm not sure if I could explain why without thinking about it harder than I've got the capacity for right now.

"That's one of the roughest easy times we've ever had, huh?" he asks, pretend casual, coming and leaning against the car. I offer him my cigarettes and he takes one, leans over to light it off mine.

"Sure was."

Nicolai comes over too, offers a flask. I take it, then look at him and laugh, and he looks hurt. "What?"

"You just climbed up on some roof to maybe-snipe somebody in a suit."

"Oh, well yes. Why would I have gotten changed?" He watches me take a swig, glancing at Butler.

"You're right, silly me." I take another swig, hand the flask to Butler. "Where'd you drop the other agent?

Butler shrugs. "By some museum that wasn't open. Funny they don't teach any of these people how to get outta zip ties, isn't it?"

"Sure is." I remember that from our brief encounter with Homeland. "You'd figure it'd be standard by now."

"You'd figure," Butler agrees.

"So you know about Bits's further plan?" He hesitates. "Butler."

"Yeah. We were operating on hypotheticals, but yeah."

"Fair enough." I drop my cigarette, check the time. Not an hour, but whatever, Bits can tell me to wait or she can tell me the plan. "I'm not mad."

"I didn't say you were." He looks at Nicolai, who takes his flask back.

"I will see if Bits is ready for us or not," he says, putting his hands in his pockets and walking inside.

"You okay?" Butler asks.

"Let's not start that again," I say.

"I meant the obvious but also, I guess you probably don't even feel the cut under your eye." He reaches out and rubs a thumb along my cheekbone gently. It stings then; it didn't register before though. Too much else going on.

"Bristol must've caught me with a ring or something," I say, and let him sit with however he wants to think about that statement.

"I guess she must've," he says, and Nicolai reappears in the entrance and waves. "He could've texted."

"Nicolai likes the personal approach, clearly." I hop off the car. Proof of concept, I can move like normal. "Plus he's probably on his way to raid one of the mini bars for our war room."

"Can't tell if that's a great thought or the worst thought."

"Right? Every time." I grin at him and we go inside to find Bits. The curtain ties are still on the chair, and it feels like we were in this room both thirty seconds ago and three years ago at the same time.

Nicolai has just poured a drink, and Bits has a fresh pitcher of that fucking coffee, and looks up at Butler and I for a second. "You both have retinal upgrades, right? From the program? Does it let you see AR?"

"I mostly keep that part of it turned off," I say. "Except for your texts, and if I need to snipe." The letting me see in the dark part has been the most useful.

"Well turn it on so I can show you the hotel where the agency is." I do the blink pattern that makes that happen. There's not a lot of ambient AR here in the hotel anyway, Bristol's old fashioned like that. It's not like when you walk down a city street and get popup ads for businesses and government weather alerts and whatnot.

The hotel is I don't know how many stories tall, but what Bits has illuminated isn't up past the first floor; it's the entrances, and then it's sublevels, done wireframe style so we can see the rooms and things. I never took much time to think about whether there were many basements here, commonly, but I'm pretty sure it isn't common to have multiple sublevels. "Shit," I say.

"Stairs and an elevator," she says. "I think Miller was telling the truth about how many agency members are here, they don't have the area super populated, and it could be that a couple of allied agencies sort of share this office space. Maybe British too? French? I don't know. But there are eleven people now, so that's Harding, the nine other agents, and Will."

"To be clear, Miller being the other guy?" I ask, nodding to the now-empty chair.

"Yeah."

"How do you know how many people are in the espionage basement?" Butler asks.

"The wifi." He looks at me and I shrug; Bits sighs. "You can use the signal to see people in a room, essentially. Easier than looking at every device location, once I've got the network."

"Fair enough," he says.

"Whiskey?" Nicolai asks, and Butler nods and I shake my head, looking at the hotel.

"Okay, so the back here is employees? And that leads to the stairs that go down-down?" I sort of trace the path with my finger.

"No, the employee entrance doesn't. The guest stairs do, here." Bits blinks it. "So if you go in the front lobby, and then past the desk and the elevators, you can take the stairs down like, a half level, before they've got a smart lock on it, which I know you know how to handle. Or you can take the elevator down, I think I've got a set of keys for that model, but—"

"But I don't want to ding on the floor and let everybody know I'm there," I finish. I look at the floating hotel, look at the flights of stairs. Nine agents, plus Harding. How surprised could they possibly be, right? Hotel full of civilians upstairs. Very full, actually.

"What's with the crowd, all vacationers?"

"There's a bachelorette party, a couple of families on separate vacations, some kind of sightseeing tour that's got a bus parked nearby, and..." Bits trails off a second, still reading the check in log or whatever, I assume. "A group of five U.S. Army on furlough from Spain."

"Actual Army, or Agency under another name?"

"Actual Army, as far as I can tell. Their records aren't this-week or even this year new."

I nod a little. I reach over and take Butler's drink and knock it back. "Okay, so I can't go in dressed like this, then."

"Why are you acting like you're doing this alone?" Butler asks. He's smart, he doesn't ask me why I'm acting like I'm doing it at all. The cost of stopping me, or trying to stop me, outweighs the benefit. Or it doesn't; Butler doesn't give a fuck about like, Bristol's happiness. He never met Will before three days ago or whenever. He wants *me* to be okay. So we kinda daisy chain those motivations together.

"We insert two people, that means we need to get three out instead of two."

He frowns. "Yeah. Obviously." That's how math works, Dolly, he doesn't say.

"If you weren't here, I'd do it alone." Well, I'd do it with Bristol holding the entire hotel ballroom in the palm of her charismatic fucking hand but I ain't exactly got that option right now. She's got too many people out there jockeying to spend time with her to just take her away again, mysteriously, and then have mysterious shit go down at a hotel downtown. She needs to keep the party people occupied.

"But I *am* here and so's Nicolai and—"

The door opens, and Suzette walks in and stops short with a look on her face that she didn't expect *anybody* to be here, much less all of us. But then her eyes hit Nicolai and she just lights up. "I've been looking for you!" she exclaims. "Is this where you've been hiding the whole time? With Bristol's friends?" She hesitates a little over friends; she doesn't really understand why Bristol has us here. What we are.

"I got caught up in conversation, I did not mean to abandon you," Nicolai says.

"De rien, but it's almost dinner, you must come." She walks towards him with her hand out, and he looks at Butler and then me apologetically, and I give him a nod.

"Go enjoy," I say. It'll be good to leave him here, embedded in the party. Worst case already happened, with all of us on deck. I'm gonna have everybody's attention in a little while here.

"If you need anything from my room, you are welcome to it," he says, as Suzette pulls him out the door. What a romcom-ass thing to happen.

"Dolly," Butler says, when the door closes behind them again.

"I'm going to need you, yes, but I need you outside to extract me, us, if I need backup. We'll only get one fuckup on this. Maybe. And I'm gonna need you to help me get ready, so if you've got this map committed to memory, meet me in my room in..." I think how long it'll take me to get from here, to Bristol's room, and then back to mine. "Fifteen."

He's still just looking at me and I can hear the seconds ticking away on a cosmic level, and then he sighs, which says everything that he's leaving unsaid. "Okay."

"Dolly?" Bits asks, frowning.

"You too. I'm just very aware of how not-private this room is."

Chapter Eleven

I grab two of Bristol's spraycan dresses in case we fuck up the first one, and because my sizing and hers ain't exactly the same, we'll need the extra for my height at the very least. I look at her shoes for a second, but we're not the same size in those, I'll just wear my boots and like, put a belt on, and it'll be fashion or some shit. I also take one of her dragonscale camisoles; I might not be doing this in an armored jacket or with a helmet, but I'd like *some* protection for my insides. I think about grabbing some of her makeup, but learning how to contour a broken nose isn't something I really got the time or interest for.

As I'm leaving, I notice the water glasses that she has with a pitcher, and something about their size and shape makes me take one. We'll see if it matches up with what Nicolai brought.

I go back through the secret passages to the opening nearest my room, listen to make sure it's all clear, and then step out. Mr. Squeak is trundling past and pauses to give me a once-over, but I pass the sniff test and she keeps going.

In my room, Bits is sitting on the bed up near the pillows, and Butler put down towels and then laid out guns and a few other fun things. "Just like Christmas," I say. I throw an eye on them, but there isn't anything I'll be able to covertly take. I could just use the active camo to get in, but that'll be better served on Butler for his covert positioning, and Bits for hers if she comes with,

110

and while I happily stole Bristol's spray cans I can't make myself borrow her active camo. I'd spend the whole time catastrophizing about what if something happens while we're doing this cowboy bullshit and she needs it and doesn't have it and then it's like an even sadder ending for Gift of the Magi.

"What the fuck is that?" Butler asks, jutting his chin out at the spray cans. He's digging in his bag for something else.

"A dress, once you're done with me," I say. "Bitsy, avert your eyes or whatever." She shrugs and pulls her headset on again.

"A *dress*?"

"Wild, right? I did it for Bristol last night, which means it's pretty idiot proof." I search on my phone a couple of times, trying to imagine what words she would've used, and come up with not the same picture but a similar one. I don't need to fuck around with sleeve straps, I would like a slit in the skirt for mobility, but if Bristol can get it done with a combat knife, I guess we can too. I drop my clothes on the floor, pull on the dragonscale camisole. "You can do that right?"

"Pull that up, I want to wrap your ribs first." He's got a roll of compression stuff, that's what he was after in his bag.

"I didn't say anything about my ribs."

"You can't hardly stand up straight."

"God, are you and Bristol gonna bond over my posture?" But I pull up the camisole to give him access, stand myself up straight as I can, then the rest of the way, hissing as I do it. He frowns, and I wonder if he's gonna pull something to keep me from going after all. He doesn't, though, he just wraps me up good and careful, and I'm glad he does it, I'm breathing easier once he's done. He pulls the camisole down over it, then picks up my phone to look at the picture I found.

"Stay still I guess," Butler says dubiously, shaking the can. I laugh, because I know exactly how he feels. Well maybe not exactly; he and I have a history of relations. Bristol was right though, it is cold coming out of the can, and it's funny to feel my skin ripple and goosebump the way I saw hers do. I stay as still as I'm able, which is pretty still actually, with my enhanced sniper training, and when he gets down to right after the camisole hem he says, "It's leaving a line there, does that matter?"

"Go over it again to make it look on purpose or something, and I'm gonna wear a belt." I've seen Bristol wear a belt over a dress, it's fine. He kinda grunts as he keeps going. The can peters out not very far past my hips and he shakes the next one.

"This is like actual witchcraft."

"Ain't it, though?" He glances up at me and I grin down. Funny it's the dress in a can that makes me and him nervous, not wound care. "Alright I guess right at the knee, to at least kinda hide the gun. Don't suppose you can do pockets?" The *look* he gives me. I pull the knife, picture how Bristol did it, and have him hold the skirt taut while I cut the slit. I roll my shoulders a little, gauging each pain as I feel the fabric curing against my skin.

"Fit okay?"

"How the fuck should I know?" I do a slow turn in front of the mirror; I guess it looks okay. I feel like I'm looking at a weird copy of myself; Bristol will be sorry that she missed Dolly-dress-up. A white dress, Jesus. I put my boots on, and especially with the compression bandaging can bend just fine, like it's real clothes, the only limitations are my own. I put a belt on and I can't tell if it looks bad, but I need to keep my extra mags somewhere. It's been a good long time since I've strapped a gun to my thigh, and even then it was because I was wearing shorts and test driving the principle, but with the length the skirt is, it's pretty hidden. I lean into the mirror, to do my signature short work with some eyeliner. I should've iced the nose. "Oh goddamn it, my hair." Maybe I should cut it. No, I don't want to take too much more time.

"Need me to watch a video on that too?" Butler asks, joking but serious, we're in ops mode. He's snapping a little first aid trauma kit on my belt. It'll have those foaming things in it that plug up bullet holes best, probably a couple of painkiller slap patches. I think about starting with one of those going, but it's only gonna get worse. I'm good, but fully expect to get shot at least once.

"If you can." I'm mostly joking, and he's picking up my phone again. "No, I don't have pins or anything, I'm just gonna twist it back into a bun and that'll be good enough for government work."

"Okay." He looks at the guns he laid out, and packs up one of the 3D printed sniper rifles that he brought from Hong Kong.

I didn't look at it enough to say what makes it different from factory, but we've all got our gun particulars. Some of what's there is what Nicolai brought, and it takes three seconds for me to find grenades. They're flashbangs, but a compact kind that looks enough like a normal frag grenade that I think it's going to work with my glass trick. I put one in carefully, just to see, and yeah, it's the right shape that the crenellations on the glass will hold the hammer even after I pull the pin. So I can wander through that lobby looking like I'm holding a drink, take the stairs down, and make my entrance. Of course, flash bangs are loud, but if I had to guess, the secret sublevels of a hotel used by secret government agencies are probably real damn sound proof. We'll find out together. "Here, I've got something else that'll probably be useful," Butler says, voice a little gruff, pulling me out of my focus.

"What is it?"

He pulls a square leather case out of his duffel; it looks like one of the jewelry boxes that Bristol uses for a necklace, broad and a couple inches deep. He opens the lid and holds it out to me, and I put the glass down to look. It's an antique derringer, big enough for four shots, small enough to drop into the top of the dress and not be a bother. Smooth wooden grips, bronze frame, you can even still read Colt etched into the top of the barrel. "It's perfect, it's like you knew," I say, picking it up and turning it over in my hands. There's an inset in the case, for a little box that's rattling with rounds, and I load it and then take the ammo box too. It's bad luck to assume you won't be able to reload.

"Just had a feeling," he says, elaborately casual, and of course I know there's more at play here, but we don't have the time.

"Thank you," I say, and kiss him. He kisses me back, but doesn't know where to put his hands, resting them on my hips after a sec. Then I load the derringer and drop it between my boobs like a dance hall girl. Alright, one last thing. I take a deep breath that's got two and a half hitches in it. "Bitsy, gonna need you to reactivate me."

She yanks her headset off and stares at me for three seconds too long. "Dolly, no." I've never heard her sound like that either. What a day of firsts this is.

"I know I said that I didn't want the full array ever again, but if I have to wade through ten or more people like a video game level, I need that buffer." Some of the super soldier programming stuck, is just permanent, like how my pain tolerance is almost completely rewired, like how my reflexes are better, but the other stuff, the stuff that we went to decommissioned bunkers looking for because it was only on paper...it's past what I can achieve just naturally, which is part of the point. It's only gonna be nine or ten people, if I get down there the way I have it pictured in my head, but that's still nine or ten *people*. That's more than I've handled, post-deprogramming. With or without another fresh injury.

"Dolly, think about how they'll consider that you've done that. You don't want them to use a codeword and turn you against us."

"That's always been the risk, right?" I grin at her. Behind me, Butler's slapping a mag into a handgun. Too bad we don't have one of their choppers, that would and wouldn't help with this. The possibility of air support tends to be nice. "You said you changed it, though, so we've got failsafes?"

"I mean, of course I have, but we haven't tested anything to see if it would work. What if I'm wrong, and nothing changes? It just textbook reactivates your super soldier suite, controls and all, and that's that?"

"Then I guess I need earplugs too."

"Dolly, I don't want to do this."

"It'll be worse for me if you don't." I can do it anyway, I think. This ain't my first rodeo, first blood, any of that. It's been us and them for so long, I can do it. Maybe I won't have to kill all of them, maybe the flashbang will be good enough and I can move fast enough. But if I don't, then we're back at square one, with the agency still knowing where we are and wanting to stop us or control us or both.

I watch her process this, watch her eyes move as she's reading stuff in AR. Doin' the math, I guess. Potential unfriendlies, how much ammo I can carry, how much psychological damage any of us might have to reckon with...it's a lotta math, but Bits is good at that kind of thing. I am very aware of the passage of time, of all of us breathing, of the party people outside. Finally, she says, "Okay. Okay earplugs over your earbuds, so you can still hear me."

"Of course."

"I'm going to reactivate you, but I'm also going to program the new failsafe word, just in case what we did to remove the control command didn't work."

"Good, yes, do it." I'm glad Bits is being careful, really I am. That's a worst-case, that Harding takes control and gives me an attack dog kill command and I take everybody out. We never wanted that possibility to exist.

It's kinda the nature of activation/deactivation that you don't really know it's happened. You don't remember those couple minutes surrounding the key phrases, as the posthypnotic suggestion comes online, or shuts down. We saw it with Will just a couple days ago, and even though I think that I'm watching this time, I know what to look for, no I don't. Butler's shrugging into his armored jacket and he's got a keffiyeh that I know messes with digital surveillance, and I check my ammo, shove a knife in my boot, and pick up the glass with the grenade in it. Bits is watching me closely, as worried as I've ever seen her.

"I feel okay," I say, and I do. This is the right choice, the right move. Hopefully no civilian collateral. That lobby full of partyers worries me. Hopefully our team all walks away from this, plus Will. I guess I gotta consider him our team now, we wouldn't really do this for anybody else. Our side, anyway.

"Butler has your active camo?" I don't remember talking about it. Butler nods, though. He isn't frowning but I recognize his deliberately-not-frowning face.

"Let's get this show on the road," I say. "They don't need too much time to either plan their exit or think about if we're coming for them."

"They have to expect we are," Bits says. She looks at Butler, who shrugs.

"Not if they think they already won."

"Hmm," Bits says, but we go out to the car. Nobody sees us, or says anything. I half hope Bristol does see us, wants to know what we're doing, wants to come along, but actually I'm glad to not have to worry about her more right now. If they think they won, then Nicolai, and Marge, and Floyd and Joker and the robot dogs are enough. And if this goes well, then for a little while anyway, we really won't need to worry about more. If it goes bad enough, I won't be worrying about anything anymore anyway.

———————

When they drop me off in front of the hotel, other people are also getting dropped off, so it's easy for me to fall into the loose groups walking into the automatic doors, keeping my eyes peeled as I cross the lobby. The people at the front desk are looking at everybody who enters, but not in a way that bothers me, they're just keeping general track of the crowd. It's gotta be hard with all that's going on, to try and mark who you think is *supposed* to be here, who you think is gonna be a problem, all of that. I bump one of the bachelorette partygoers, or more correctly, she's blasted out of her mind and bumps me. She doesn't even look at me, just kind of exclaims something and moves in the opposite direction. Some of those girls are carrying on, or trying to, with what looks to me like some of the army guys, who've somehow been on base long enough to forget what partying girls like this look like. Or maybe they didn't know before now, and their horizons are being abruptly broadened.

Then one of the army guys backs up into me, as the story he's telling gets too big for the space he's in, hard enough that I let out an involuntary gasp and come real close to dropping my grenade glass. Good thing the pin's still in, but it'd still fuck the situation for that to go spinnin' across the floor.

"Sorry, oh god sorry, I didn't see you there," the guy says, the kind of red-faced and pale-lidded that says he's both sunburned and also drunker than he feels yet and both of those are gonna suck come morning. He grabs at my elbow and there's too many people I still need to get past to do anything so I let him do it, keeping my glass in the other hand away from him. I can barely hear him but it's fine, I can read lips pretty good by this point.

"It's okay it's really crowded," I yell, grinning hard and blinking a lot. Can't say I've ever wanted to pretend to be drunk before.

He lights up like it's Christmas. "You're American!" Oh come on.

"Yeah! But I have to..." He's still got my elbow, is trying to explain to his friends that he found another American, and I look 'em over real quick. One is stone cold sober and hates this, but he must hate leaving people unsupervised worse. The others are also very drunk, maybe with some other additives, and they forgot him and his story the second he broke the circle and ran into me. He can't get their attention back, but the sober one looks at me. Thank Christ for the bachelorettes, he's mentally prepped to think I'm one of them, or in that category, and not anything more interesting. Or more threatening, if Harding tagged him as some kind of frontline here. Interagency cooperation, son, just need you to keep a casual lookout. Maybe that's why he's sober, maybe not. He's strapped and the other ones aren't. But his eyes slide off me and my spraycan dress without registering.

"Kevin, you asshole, you can't go grabbing random girls, I don't care where she's from."

"Shit, I'm sorry!" Kevin looks at me again, wide-eyed, and I hold up my free hand.

"It's okay! Have fun!" Kevin says something else that I can't hear, as I weave into the crowd away from him. Nobody else takes particular notice of me, and I tell myself it's because I did this stupid dress thing to blend in, instead of coming in here actually geared. Probably it's what kept the sober Army guy from keying in. I changed my silhouette to not look like an operator.

I wait until I'm in the stairwell to pull the pin on the grenade and settle it back down into the cup. I just wear the ring on my thumb, I might get a chance to wave it at somebody for intimidation purposes. I might just drop the glass as my opening sally. We'll see.

The smart lock is no trouble, it's not one I can slap, but it is one that has the manual bypass right there and visible under a little rubber plug, and I shim it quick and am through that door and pulling it softly closed behind me in under a minute. Some vulnerabilities just never get fixed.

This flight of stairs goes for a while. Down, turn at a landing, down. Extra secure, extra quiet. No, upstairs isn't gonna hear this grenade, or any gunshots. Another reason not to take the elevator, though. They're finicky, and return to a ground floor and then open and lock and that's that, if a fire alarm goes off or whatever. Maybe I should've pulled one on my way in, but that's also the opposite of stealthy ain't it.

The door at the bottom of the stairs has a keycard reader and a number pad, I guess so you can use either. I run the card we took off that other guy. Miller? If they're smart they would've deactivated it. The reader goes green and the door clicks. Or it's a trap. I don't pull the gun yet, I just inch the door open and have a peek. Nothing, nobody. It's so quiet down here that if I'm not careful I can hear my rough-edged breathing. My fingertips are zinging, I'm so hyped up. I close the door behind me quiet as I can, listening to see if anybody reacts to the click. Nothing. There's a camera in the hall here but I can't think about that, gotta trust that Bitsy has it in hand. She always does.

It's too quiet, maybe they cleared out already. Or they're used to the quiet and waiting. Or it's the fucking earplugs but I made a promise and I do my best to keep those. Nine Agents. Harding. Will. One of them's gonna be Clancy, so I guess we'll get a tiebreaker. I run the map in my head, of where people were when Bits showed us, and clear the first two rooms I pass without anything and then the third has a guy in a vest and BDUs and those yellow sunglasses and he was ready for me but also he shifts right as I get to the door and I hear his belt creak.

Ready or not, I'm faster than a normal guy like that can be, and I clear the gun from my thigh holster, pop the door the rest of the way open by stomping right next to it, and put a round in the space between his collarbones before he's finished drawing. He looks surprised; they often do. I get the rest of the way into the room, swing the door half shut again, fade back into the corner, crouch, wait. The sound of a firearm should be unmistakable to these people. There should be immediate response.

And there is. They're methodical, they've gotta assume this guy is already down. I hear their boots and can envision them funneling out of the nearby rooms to come to this one, giving a hand signal to hold outside, then somebody presses the door open with a rifle butt and I throw my glass past them, so it hits the wall across the hallway, and I close my eyes and duck my head under my forearm. The glass breaks, they startle, the flash-bang goes off, they give muffled yells. One fires, I think they just involuntarily squeezed off a round, and one staggers in front of the doorway and I drop them. Another, in a crouch, comes to check them and I drop him too. Then I leave my corner and enter the hallway, shooting the woman who's still standing, first in the shoulder, then in the chest.

There's one on the ground against the wall, face bloody from sprayed glass looks like, and he shoots me in the belly twice before I steal a breath and put both hands on my gun for the first time and headshot him.

Then it's quiet again. Four Agents. Harding. Will. Nine rounds left in this mag, maybe that's enough and I won't need to reload. Maybe I should reload now, to be sure. Decisions, decisions.

I check myself; something cut one of my arms, maybe just fragments, not a lot of blood, doesn't hurt. My stomach hurts but the dragonscale caught the rounds for me. If that one had a rifle it would've punctured, I think. It'll bruise up nice later. Join whatever my ribs are doing.

//Are you okay?// Bits asks. It must've cost her a lot to break silence.

It feels like it's definitely me having that thought, but it's behind glass, like me and my actions are over here, and everything that I think and feel and remember are over there. I don't remember this feeling; the first time I got programmed, I was then in boot, and didn't have time to think and feel and remember.

"Yeah," I say, so quietly I can't hear myself. Butler doesn't say anything but it's like I can *feel* him listening.

I stalk down the hall, posted up, ready. I gotta assume the four agents left are the gold star ones, because if what they sent first was the front line, then they should already be surrendering or they just got a death wish. I gotta assume that Harding is no slouch. I guess he could just be an ROTC-officer school deskjockey, but I'm not so sure that's the case. I know now that

Clancy's an operator. The hallway empties into a bigger, open room. Empty. Stairwell door across the way. Wishing I brought a second flashbang. The glass was a good trick, though. I drop mag, reload. If the next ones have more consistent armor I'm gonna need more shots.

I edge the stairwell door open and it seems clear all the way down. No noise, no shadows, no gun oil other than what I brought with me. I go down, step by step, keeping my back to the wall. They could circle around on me, probably, using the elevator. I don't think they will. I get to the next door, and it's propped with a plant, like somebody wanted air. It's almost funny, maybe it's funny. I can feel the weight of people in the next room and I stop, wait. They know I'm here, if I were them, this is where I'd have a rifle set up.

I breathe, clear my thoughts, shed my tension.Then I tuck and roll low into the room, come up on a knee and snap my gun into place, get one guy center mass, probably his vest took it, and the one with the rifle takes the shot a little too soon and it goes through the bicep of my left arm. The cybernetic stuff is sorta self healing, to a point. One round is fine. That arm's more than paid for itself today. I feel the shockwave, but it doesn't *hurt* and now that I've seen the rest of the room I can duck to the side for cover, such as it is, behind one of those movable cubicle partitions. The guy I shot is grumbling about his vest and the woman with the rifle tells him to shut up and I listen to their voices and decide that they've for some reason decided not to move and pop out again, double tap the guy I shot the first time, and risk taking my time aiming up on the woman with the rifle before I shoot.

We fire at the same time, and her round grazes right past my face, and my round hits her scope. She drops but I'm not sure she's down and I cross the room in the blink of an eye and kick both their weapons away. Yeah. Good enough.

Why am I not picking up weapons as I go? I want to do this fast, and I don't want to make the mistake of relying on anything one of their hackers can turn off on me, since these are all smart guns. Actually, since they're all smart guns, they might not even work for me unless I talk to 'em with a paperclip or wait for Bits to jailbreak them and I don't have the *time*.

Two left, then Harding. Will.

Chapter Twelve

Another set of stairs, this time they've got a tripwire set that I spot just in time, quarter way up from the bottom. I back up, consider. I look over the railing, gauge the distance, and just go over that and drop down. I land okay, but I'm also not the most stealthy and one of them rushes me, gets me in the sternum with his shoulder and runs me into the wall under the stairs. Unfortunately for him, closer isn't safer, and I ride the momentum, yell-exhale on impact, then stomp his instep when he goes to reposition. The angle's bad, I don't think I broke anything the way I intended, but it doesn't feel good, and he jerks back and bends a little and I grab a handful of his hair and use that momentum to introduce his face to my knee, let go to let him stumble back in shock and assess his body armor, and put a round in his thigh about where I think the femoral is. The fountain tells me I'm right.

This dress isn't so white anymore.

As this is all happening, he's conveniently blocking his friend's shot, and as he's dropping I spin away to get to the side of the doorway and take cover, and the rifle coughs and clips me in the calf. I still make it but I need to handle that right now. I grab at the first aid kit, pop out one of the foam things and I break off the end of the tube as I'm shaking it, get the nozzle against the wound and the button pressed. I can hear the rifle reloading and I wonder how many shots they took, that they only got me with the one. Maybe they've just got the reflex, like when you're playing a shooter and want to be ready to fully mag dump at a moment's notice. This doesn't hurt too bad but it does hurt a lot and that guy hurt my ribs again or more or whatever and it'd be stupid not to use a pain patch, so I take the time to slap one of those on too.

I hear the scuff of a boot; are they really coming closer? They had to hear me use the foam, it makes an unmistakable noise. I look at the bright pool of blood from the other guy, tilt my head so I can see the lights going down the hallway reflected. A shadow of movement. Yeah, they're taking the time to reposition, probably if only so they're not in the same place I saw them last. That's okay, a breather is good. Let the painkiller go to work. Another boot scuff, the slightest shadow reflected in the edge of the blood. They're still a ways down the hallway.

I throw an eye over my shoulder at that tripwire to see if it was attached to anything but no. That's smart, wouldn't want to use mines or an IED down here, too close.

I'm not gonna get another hail Mary shot down somebody's scope and we're both ready for each other and I guess I just need to get a move on. I look over at the dead guy, but he's no use to me, framed in the doorway. Trying to take anything off him would be a waste of time and just get me killed.

I've still got the grenade pin on my thumb and I think about that. If the person with the rifle is like me, they know very well what the sound of that ring on concrete sounds like. Maybe it'll buy me a couple seconds. I drop the pin, do a silent three count like I'm cooking a grenade, then throw my handgun clattering down the hall, follow when I hear "Shit," and scrambling.

They didn't move very far up the hall, they were cautious, but they switched sides and now they're crouched with their back turned, so that tells me they're wearing a ballistic vest too and hoped it would save their ass. Literally. But the grenade doesn't go off, and they're turning back around as I get *almost* to my gun and I yank the derringer out of my boobs and shoot for where I see skin, clipping their wrist, and I recognize the wince and jaw set *very* well, this person was also in the program, or in *a* program and they get the rifle around and hipfire it as I dive for them and this camisole doesn't cover shit, I can't believe we let Bristol wear it for as many ops as she has but also nobody 'lets' Bristol do things.

But that pain patch is singing through me and getting shot'll put a delay on you but I've already got the momentum, so when I collide with them the rifle clatter-slides across the floor and I jam the derringer up under their jaw with my left hand and pull the trigger the three more times. Then I sit back on my heels, drop the casings, reload, my hands working without thinking, even though I can't really feel my right fingers right now. Good thing I was ambidextrous even before the program.

Despite the pain patch and the programming, it hurts enough that I'm not sure exactly where I'm hit as I jam the derringer behind my belt, pull and prep another foam thing. Right shoulder, further from my neck rather than closer, so that's good. Doesn't seem to have broken my collarbone or anything. There aren't really any good safe places to get shot unless you already got replacement limbs or unless you were wearing better protection than me, but I'll live through this one anyway, and probably not need much. I can still move the arm and flex my fingers. I think the round went clean through, I feel the foam drip down my back before it hardens. I pick my gun up off the floor, give it a quick check to make sure nothing bent or broke. It's fine.

Just Harding and Will left now.

I'm surprised Bits hasn't checked in again but maybe I don't have a good enough signal down here, can't take the time. I move down the hallway again, quiet as I can, except I think I might be leaving bloody boot prints. I can't bother about that right now. Miller told the truth about personnel, at least; I clear every room on my way to the final room, the conference room or office or whatever they did there. No sign of anybody else.

No, where's Clancy?

As I get closer to that room, I hear Harding, though. He sounds like how the Chief did anytime he dressed us down for not running a scenario right, or for being goof offs. I never think about Chief; funny what surfaces, sometimes. The doors're thick as the walls down here and the sound is dampened, but that's Harding's tone of voice, no doubt, and Will isn't saying anything. Is Harding dressing Will down? Is Harding on the horn yelling at backup that isn't coming in time? Only way to find out is to go through door number one.

I kick it open, and they're sitting at the conference table, or Will is sitting and Harding is standing and talking to him while using a knife hand instead of pointing. Pointing's bad. Will flinches less than I would've expected, guess he's learning, and Harding full body reacts, but in a way that tells me that yeah, he isn't just a deskjockey, and he turns to me like he's at ready, but he doesn't have a weapon and I don't take the shot. He made the choice to be here, and to not bar the door, and to not have a weapon. We look at each other across the expanse of the room; it can't really be all that big, but my perceptions are understandably going a little screwy right now. Still operable, just affected. I can feel the little shock-tremors that the programming just lets me ignore.

He says "Steel magnolia," and even after the gunplay and grenade and earplugs, I hear him a little too loud and clear and let out a breath, but nothing changes. This is only my third or fourth time seeing Harding, so I can't really track nuances of his expression, though I'd say 'put upon' fits the bill, at the very least.

"Are you takin' the time to dress him down before you kill him?" I ask, half laughing with disbelief and maybe delirium, and then I see the shimmer in the corner of my eye and almost turn fast enough to put a round in Clancy instead of the opposite wall. Guess Clancy isn't technically an agent, shouldn't've trusted Miller's estimate of how many agents. Wonder how Bitsy's wifi trick didn't see him though.

He knows he hurt me before, and he knows using his bulk is the best bet, and he tries to run me into the wall and I've had about enough of that today and get a grip on whatever part of him's touching me, drop to the floor. which I've also had enough of today, and use his momentum to put him up and over. We're far enough from the wall still that he doesn't hit it, but he comes crashing down on the floor, and he must've landed on his active camo box because he glitches back into sight, fades out again, then comes back for good in the time it takes me to get back to my feet in a much sloppier kip up then the one I did like an hour ago. I hear, or feel, the spray foam that I put in my leg crack. That's a new one.

But it doesn't suit my needs to give Clancy a chance to get back up again, and I reach back for the derringer because damn if I know where my other gun got to and somebody, Harding, fires a round into the ceiling. "Enough."

I back up a couple steps, slowly, with my hands visible, so I can keep an eye on both him and Clancy. Will's still in his seat, though he has turned to watch. He knew I was deprogrammed, knew Bits knew some of the nuts and bolts, and didn't warn Harding. Fucking steel magnolia indeed, come the fuck on. "Time to negotiate?" I ask. There's my gun, partway between me and Harding. He isn't holding his weapon on me, that's interesting. He's holding it on Will.

Clancy climbs slowly to his feet, leaving a puddle of plastic shards on the floor. He's frowning, looks at me, looks at Harding.

"The last time we had contract negotiations, things fell through," Harding says. "The only one who honored their agreement is Marquis."

"What can I say, somebody takes you someplace on their submarine and surrounds you with armed guards, you sign a contract that's put in front of you." I can't get over there before he shoots Will, if that's his actual intent.

"We treated you people very well."

"You did." He doesn't know what to do with that, and Clancy fidgets. I wait; I'm not the negotiator, for one, and for two, I'm not really sure what kind of compelling argument I can offer him after killing a bunch of his personnel. Plus I hate talking with earplugs in. I think Harding is doing the extended math. He might be able to shoot Will before I can do anything about it, but I'll definitely shoot him before Clancy can do anything about it.

Harding nods like he's made up his mind, or maybe he's got his directives from higher-ups, who knows. Bits has stayed out of it, which is probably for the better. "Will Scarlet is no longer a member of this agency. He was lost during an operation in Morocco. His parents will receive a letter commending him and thanking him for his service."

"That's good, his mom's real sweet. Makes good cookies too." Maybe now ain't the right time to taunt him but I also feel pretty put upon. From the swallowed-frog look on his face, he didn't know I interacted with either of his folks that night I gave his laptop back, once Bitsy was done with it. I pop my earplugs; I don't think I'll need 'em anymore. I could be wrong, but also just suddenly couldn't stand the feeling. He won't have a different codeword that works.

Harding holsters his gun, and says, "His remains will be signed over to them as well."

"May he have a comfortable afterlife or whatever," I say. My adrenaline's starting to come down, and that means a whole lotta hurt is starting to surface. Even with the pain patch and the reactivation. The painkillers Bits gave me earlier.

"As a result, his case files are being cleared and closed. We see no further threats to national security in any of his personal projects, he was simply doing his due diligence and had some bad luck."

"Could've saved us all a lotta grief," I mutter. I'm unwilling turn my back on Clancy, who seems like he'd just as soon pick up where we left off.

"Hindsight," Harding says, weight of a judge's gavel in his voice, and Will flinches, just a little. I'm sure he was also real broken up anytime his parents said that they weren't angry, just disappointed.

"If I hadn't made it to this room, would you be having the same conversation?"

"Yes, because I also wasn't interested in being on the receiving end of whatever retribution your global friends network would bring down upon us. You can have Will, he is no longer of use to us. You are clearly capable and dangerous, but in a way that does not have overlap with our jurisdictional concerns."

"Wish I had clarification on what those are, exactly," I say. I glance at Clancy, who's just shy of pouting.

"I'm sure your friend Bits can fill you in," Harding says dryly. "Now get the fuck out of my area of operation."

"Roger that." I look at Will, who's still sitting, and he's got a pretty priceless look on his face. "Take a picture, it'll last longer," I say.

"Sorry." He pushes his chair back, stands. "Mr. Harding, sir—"

Harding holds up a hand. "Get out of here, son. I hope your little blonde is worth it." I laugh, which ain't exactly the kindest thing, but also ain't that the heart of all of this. Harding gives me another onceover, again with that look on his face that speaks of missed opportunities. He actually kicks the handgun over to me. "I look forward to never seeing you again, miss."

"Right back at you." I pick it up, then stand aside to let Will go out ahead of me, before backing out of the room. I give Clancy a salute before pulling the door closed. "You want a blindfold or will you be okay?"

"I'll be okay," Will says quietly. "Thank you."

"Don't mention it. And watch your step at the bottom of these stairs." We make our way through the floors, up the stairs. I keep flexing my right hand, just to make sure I can. I haven't been hurt like this since the job where Bits got her brain scrambled. Hard to say if I'm in better shape now or not, but no that's dumb, of course I am. I'm not cruising for any limb replacements this time and my blood stayed mostly inside. I lost some, got a couple extra holes, but it's fine, we'll get that situated soon.

I slip a little, stepping over one of the bodies, and Will actually reaches out to steady me, and I let him. It's a nice impulse for him to have. Then we're in the last staircase, the first one, the long one, going up and up.

"I don't know how you're going to walk out of here looking like that," he says to me at one point.

"Yeah, good point," I say. "Hey Bits?"

//I'm here// she says. //Butler can come in and meet you at the stairs?//

//Got it covered// Butler says. I don't know what conversation they had when I was down there, but I'm glad they did, and I'm glad they left me to it. This could've been worse. Could've been better, but could've been far worse.

"Thanks," I say. Fuck, I'm thirsty. "Bring water too?"

//I remember.//

"Butler's meeting us," I say to Will. "You probably got that."

"I did." He's got kinda that dazed look that he did when we left Vegas but it's different, just a little. Like he's got a freedom now that he didn't know he wanted and doesn't know what to do with. Well. He'll figure it out. Him and Bristol. "You're going to laugh at me, but are you okay?"

"I'll need medical attention, but I think I'm unlikely to drop dead." I look down; I'm not still leaving bloody footprints, anyway. I reholster my handgun, and put the derringer back in the top of my spraycan dress, which all things considered, has really held up to what I just put it through. Other than not being white anymore.

We reach the ground floor, and the door to the outside world, and Will has a look through the little wire-grid window. "He's there," he says in a voice of strange relief, and pulls the door open. Even after all I just did for him, Will doesn't want to spend one on one time with me, which is fine. Butler pushes in, gives a short, hard sniff when he looks at me, and sheds the jacket he was wearing to put around my shoulders. It doesn't cover all of me, but it covers the worst of it, and since I foamed the leg wound early, maybe that's explainable to a casual observer as I fell and got scraped up on pavement.

Then we open the door, and cross the lobby at a leisurely pace. It's even more crowded now, and dark out now, which for some reason made the lobby lights get lowered and some kind of flashing party lighting happen. I don't really have an explanation, but it sure suits our purposes. The army guys aren't there anymore. Butler left the car right out front, and a hotel employee is standing there with a look on his face that says the car shouldn't be there and he doesn't want to have to deal with it.

"I'm moving it now," Butler says, too loud, too cheerful. "Have a good night."

"Shotgun," I say, and Butler laughs. He opens the door for me, and then stands back in between the hotel door and me, but I get myself into the car without too much trouble. I got time left on the pain patch.

At first, we don't make a whole lot of conversation on the way back. Once we're away from the hotel, Bits drops the active camo and Will about shits himself, and that's pretty funny. Other than that, he keeps his own counsel back there, and Butler keeps looking at me.

"Dolly, you need a hospital," Bits says at one point. She doesn't think I'll agree, but has to try, I get that.

"We know a guy," I say. "We'll figure it out." I can't remember where that guy might be right this second. Maybe Dubai, maybe Portugal. Portugal'd be better for our purposes. "Too bad we don't have a chopper."

"Sorry, it wouldn't fit in my bag," Butler says.

"That's fine, what you brought me was real good."

"When I saw it, I knew it was for you," he says.

I find his cigarettes in the jacket pocket, light one on my first try, so I think I look worse than I am. I missed the opportunity to mention that the blood isn't all mine.

Finally, we're back at Bristol's hotel, and Will gets out of the car almost immediately but then just stands here, like he isn't sure he's fine to go in.

"C'mere." I hold my cigarette in my teeth and straighten Will's tie and pat him on the shoulder. "Go on back to her now."

He'd been looking towards the hotel, but actually makes eye contact for once, startled. "You're not coming in?"

"Nah. Seems like I should skip it. 'Specially with the state I'm in. She'll get mad about the rugs." He looks at me a minute longer, frowning, then turns and walks across the parking lot, through the side gate. I listen, as though I'll hear Bristol see him, greet him, but the smeared murmur of voices and laughing and music mask that, of course.

"She'll forgive you," Butler says, taking the pack out of his/my pocket and lighting his own cigarette.

I shrug. "Yeah, maybe." Bits finishes extricating herself from the car and just looks plain exhausted. "When's the last sleep you got, Bitsy?"

"I'm fine," she says. "But—"

"It's all that jet fuel you've been drinking," I say. "I said you were supposed to dilute it."

"Dolly—"

"It's fine. We'll see our guy, and then I'll head back to Hong Kong with Butler, stay there awhile. You always know how to find me."

"Yeah, that's true," she says. She still looks worried. *And* exhausted. "Let me deactivate you again first?"

"Oh yeah, true, good." I take a breath. "This is gonna suck so bad."

"Maybe come in and—"

"Butler, can you pack our stuff?"

"Yeah, I'll get that squared away, and call Doc. Can you wait until I'm back at least?"

"We can wait," I say, and he saunters off. "See, that wasn't so bad?"

"I'm not validating that," Bits says, shaking her head. "We shouldn't have let you go in there alone."

I laugh. "I don't think 'let' enters into any of our decisions." She still looks dubious.

"It's just not how we typically do things. I know I won't change your mind, especially since it's already over with."

"Exactly, now we're on the same page." I let the car door hang open and sit back down on the edge of the seat, my legs dangling out. I know it's hot out, but I hug Butler's jacket around me anyway, to smell him, and in anticipation of what it's gonna feel like when Bits drops my programming again.

I finish my cigarette, and kind of whistle aimlessly and tunelessly until Butler comes back out with our duffles. "Leaving most of the arsenal for Marge," he says, "So I took a minute to let her know. We can always just print more. Said goodbye to Nicolai too."

"Oh good. We know how he worries." Bits makes a noise like an outraged sigh. "You ready Bitsy?"

"The question is if you're ready. Did you already call your 'guy'?" she asks, turning to Butler.

"Yeah, and he put me in touch with somebody in town, so we can go right there and get her stable and get the good drugs. Get some sleep. Then make travel arrangements."

"I can do that part," Bits says.

"Sounds good," I say.

Bits puts her finger in front of her face, between us, and has me focus on it. There's a tone that she plays in my ears, I remember that, and then there's other parts that I don't remember, and then those pieces of glass keeping things separate fall away, and all the pain is a brief roaring haze and maybe I'll just black out but no, I get my breathing under control and push it down some. Those pain patches I already slapped on make that possible, I think. I blink and look around. Bits is still standing there, still frowning. Butler's crouched in next to me, though, like he wants to comfort me somehow but there's no good way to go about it.

"Okay, all set," Bits says.

"Thanks, Bitsy, you're the best." I manage a grin at her, and she quirks her lips and shakes her head.

"Just try to be careful, okay?"

"I do what I can," I say. "That sounds like I'm lying, I'm not lying. Anyway, I'm sure I'll see you in a couple months. It won't be long."

"It probably won't be long, yeah." She stands there long enough to watch Butler help me sit right in the car and buckle me in, and then she turns and goes into the hotel.

He gets in the driver's seat and starts the car. "You're unbelievable," he says.

"If you're gonna get on my case about—"

"No, I mean, what you just accomplished. You could've been killed and instead you're...well you're in rough shape but okay. And all for Bristol?"

"Friendship is like that sometimes," I mutter.

"Right, yeah, the power of friendship." He doesn't roll his eyes, but he might as well have.

"Fuck you."

"Not now, but once we're back in Hong Kong you'll probably be up for it again."

Epilogue

B utler proposes on the ferry over to Hong Kong. He doesn't have a ring, but that's not a surprise. Neither of us is in a hurry for a degloving accident. That's what the derringer was for, a pretty little thing, if somebody was inclined to get me in particular something that's pretty. Plus it is *very* functional, and what more could a girl ask for.

"Last time, it wasn't the right time," he says. "Maybe it isn't now either. I even did it right, I went and talked to your parents first."

"My parents love you," I say. We're alone on the deck, of course, because he's got a lick of sense. Between the guys we knew, I got pretty well patched up in Morocco and still have some pain but it's manageable without hard drugs, even. "That sounds like I'm hedging. I love you."

"But?"

"But...hell, I don't know. I just want to understand, I guess? What do we need to be married for, if we understand each other? Just want to stake your claim?" I knew this was coming, or suspected it was coming, but I still have to ask.

"Would that be wrong?" I wait and he laughs. "It could just be for the hell of it, could be so I can legally leave you all my assets, if I die in a terrible 3D printed helicopter crash."

"We don't need to be married for that."

"I suppose not." He reaches over and takes my hand. My real hand. He's maybe the most serious I've ever seen him and we've seen some serious shit. Recently, even. "You're the person I want to spend my days with. That I never get tired of. That I think about all the time."

I'm not surprised. I can't possibly be surprised. I've told him no or put him off every other time and still he waits and then asks again. To be fair, it's been years; since before I started working with Bits and Bristol. And we've spent a lot of time apart over those years. And a lot of close time together just these past couple days, and every time, it's like we pick up exactly where we left off. "Butler, I don't know."

"You already said that." He glances past me, just a split second, but I turn and look; members of the ferry crew are suddenly acting very casual.

"Did you pick here to propose so that the captain would marry us?" I ask.

He hesitates. "Maybe."

"Bristol would be furious if she missed my wedding," I say, as if I think that bridge isn't burned. Maybe it isn't. There's only so mad she stays for so long. Plus, we fixed it. There'll be another job, soon enough.

"Is that enough to get you to say yes?" He grins.

"It'd be shitty for you if it was," I say.

"But?" He knows. He knew before he asked, this time.

"Yeah, let's do it."

Butler gives the crew the thumbs up, and the ferry blares its horn. Wait 'til I send Bitsy the pictures.

PREVIEW

Run With the Hunted 7: The Casino Job

Chapter One

When we are discussing a job, it is very rare for one of us to just outright say no; in fact, I'm not certain it has ever happened. There's all manner of back and forth about feasibility and approach, but when one of us brings a job to the table, we've always looked at it as a yes, if perhaps qualified. This time, Bits says no.

I am *extremely* surprised. I pause mid sentence, having just said "casino." Bits is frowning and blinking as though she is *very* alarmed and had perhaps only been half listening before I said that particular word.

Our new colleagues, Perry and Garnet have only done two very small, very easy jobs with us, and they look at each other uneasily, Perry laughing nervously. They stop when they see me looking.

I take a sip of sparkling water, refocus on Bits. "I'm sorry, darling, I hadn't finished speaking yet. Perhaps you can explain why you are saying no?"

"We aren't doing a casino job," she says. "Even a year ago, we wouldn't have." Her eyes dart briefly to Perry and Garnet but for a different reason than I looked at them. She eloquently, to me, means their lack of experience and lack of time with us.

Garnet takes it as entreaty for support, and looks between us. "Well why don't we hear Bristol out? Maybe we could do a casino job?" She smiles at me, seeking approval. Garnet is particularly disposed to my way of doing things, taking a social situation in hand and steering it in one's favor.

"If Bits says no..." Perry starts dubiously, then shrugs. "I don't know, casino jobs are a big deal, aren't they?"

"Yes, they are," Bits says, her eyes still too wide.

"Oh, I see, I've simply given the wrong impression! I don't mean a *traditional* casino job, darling, we won't be taking *their* money. "Look at this exhibition! All of these art pieces covered in all of those diamonds." I pull out my phone, gauche in conversation, but I forward the exhibition announcement to Bits. "And the casino is right in town." Town being Paris.

"I thought we learned our diamonds lesson last time?" But her eyes are unfocused, looking at the information. Perry and Garnet exchange a look; they've heard about the diamonds job, of course, anybody in our sort of profession has heard scraps and whispers of it. It caused quite the ripple in the ecosystem, even though that was not our intent.

"We know how to handle them much better, yes. And can't you scout them, make sure that they are exactly what meets the eye? There are ever so many articles about the artist." I could put on a much more wheedling tone, but I'm certain Bits won't notice either way. Such nuance is not Bits's area of expertise, and it does not sway her. "Marquis is the one who told me about the exhibit, and who mentioned they might perhaps know at least one buyer who would like these items intact, thus we would not be handling the diamonds individually."

Bits is quiet for a long time, thinking I presume, or looking up that information. Then she says, "What's the play, then? How do you think we're going to go into the casino and take what isn't theirs but is very much covered under their security umbrella?"

"According to at least one article I've read, they manually place a protective cowl over each piece every night, and then shift them around, to create the illusion that they've move when nobody is watching. Then other staff unveil them in the morning."

"So you think that we'll insert, posed as the art staff, and instead of shuffling them around..."

"Shuffle them right off the floor to a waiting vehicle, yes." Perry perks up at that, but doesn't interrupt. They are very focused on vehicles, every aspect of vehicles. Operating, maintaining, enhancing. But Bits is quiet again, and though I have the unusual impulse to continue explaining myself, and pleading the case for this job, I wait. Bits has her own calculations to make, and is forever ferreting out information even as we speak. Garnet fidgets, looking at me, and picks up her drink instead. We are meeting at my apartment, which is only one floor above street level, and the evening traffic outside of the window has already tapered off.

Will is occupying himself in the little library that we've built. I enjoy the library for the way all of the book spines are pleasing to the eye; he enjoys the library for the pleasure of selecting the books at the old booksellers that we go past on our walks, for taking in knowledge that he otherwise would not have found, for the escape that novels allow. He does not particularly care to involve himself in our criminal pursuits; indeed, they still seem to pain him. I've told him that there is no shame in stealing from rich people, who have earned nothing, but he isn't able to embrace that philosophy. Perhaps one day. He's still becoming accustomed to this life, to his freedom.

"We aren't doing something like this without Dolly," Bits says finally.

"Without *Dolly*." In all of our association, Bits of all people has never caught me socially unawares. I ought to have expected this, though. There's been a Dolly shaped hole in our life these months now, nearly a year, and we simply do not address it. Perry's eyes widen; if Garnet is a bit of a baby duckling to me, Perry seems to have a near-worshipful regard for Dolly, though it is impossible to tell how they might have heard of Dolly in the first place. Our reputations precede us, always.

"If we're going to do something that even vaguely resembles a casino job, even if it isn't anything to do with the casino's own money, I want Dolly to be with us. We need her abilities and experience. So I guess it's a qualified no."

"It isn't as though you're asking for the *impossible*." I sip my water again, my last memories of Dolly coming to mind as though they'd been eager for the opportunity. Her bundling me into the car away from Will, me swearing I would never forgive her if she did exactly that. Slapping her in the face. And then her saying exactly the right thing to make sure I straightened myself up and returned to the party with my facade intact. That was it. I never even thanked her, once Will showed up at my side again two hours later. His facade is less unshakeable than mine, but I have also never been able to get him to tell me what happened.

"She hasn't been working," Bits says. Bits also never told me what happened.

"Perfect, I'll just go to...wherever she is, and whisk her away back to us." I am certain that simply calling her will not be appropriate, it must be in person.

"Hong Kong."

"Oh, is she there with Butler? Perhaps he can be entreated to join us as well." A range of emotions swiftly crosses Bits's face, so swiftly that I am not prepared to parse or interpret them. I spend so much time not needing to read her flat affect that it did not occur to me that I would have to be prepared to. This is indeed troublesome, or at the very least perplexing.

She shrugs. "Probably not."

"Hong Kong? Bristol, you're going alone?" Garnet asks, trying not to sound too eager, the sweet girl.

"I'm afraid that I will, darling, it will be simpler and swifter that way. I could travel professionally, were I to ever give the rest of this up."

"Did I hear Hong Kong?" Will asks, appearing in the doorway and pausing when he sees us gathered.

"Yes, darling, I'm going to take a quick little trip to see Dolly. You won't even notice that I'm gone."

"Of course I'll notice," he says, but he's got the shadow of a frown on his face. "Did she invite you? Does she know you're coming?"

"Well, I mean for it to be a surprise, but I'm certain Bits will do what she feels best in that regard. I give myself into her hands." I look from Will to Bits, who has a distinct 'arranging travel plans' look on her face. "I'll just be there and back again, no need to accompany me."

"If you say so." He seems about to say more, but crosses the room to the liquor cabinet instead. Dolly does put him on edge, the poor dear. "Is this to do with the job you're planning?"

"It is, yes."

He nods, mixing himself a gin and tonic. "Anybody else?" he asks the room. He knows that if I wanted a drink, I would not have the water.

"Yes, thank you," Garnet says. Perry shakes their head, and Bits almost never drinks alcohol and is not part of that equation. He hands Garnet the first drink he mixed, and pours another.

"I guess just let me know if you need me," he says, coming and brushing my cheek with a kiss.

"Of course I will, darling."

"You might want to get packed." Bits says. "I can get you on a flight in three hours."

Further work by Jennifer R. Donohue

———————

Exit Ghost

The Drowned Heir

Between the Blood and the Sun

Other books in the Run With the Hunted series

Run With the Hunted

Run With the Hunted 2: Ctrl Alt Delete

Run With the Hunted 3: Standard Operating Procedure

Run With the Hunted 4: VIP

Run With the Hunted 5: Insert Coin to Play

About the Author

Jennifer R. Donohue grew up at the Jersey Shore and now lives in central New York with her husband and their Doberman. A member of the SFWA, she works at her local public library where she also facilitates a writing workshop. Her work has appeared in *Apex Magazine*, *Escape Pod*, *Fusion Fragment*, and elsewhere. Her debut novel, *Exit Ghost*, is available now. She tweets @AuthorizedMusin and you can subscribe to her Patreon for a new short story every month: https://www.patreon.com/JenniferRDonohue

Read more at https://authorizedmusings.blogspot.com/.

www.ingramcontent.com/pod-product-compliance
Lightning Source LLC
Chambersburg PA
CBHW01205150626
46549CB00023B/3199